YOURS, WITH LOVE

When Kurt Hollister mentioned to his Uncle Paul Jean that he had heard the miners' working conditions at the family gold mines in California were bad, Paul Jean welcomed the opportunity to visit the mines in person. And, of course, he took his pretty new secretary, Ellen Marshall, with him, for he had been dictating a book to her giving the history of the mines.

And Ellen, knowing that she was falling desperately in love with Kurt, was glad to go with Paul Jean. For Kurt had a wife—hard, spiteful Beatrice—who didn't love Kurt herself, but who was determined that no one else should have him.

But when Paul Jean broke his leg—almost as soon as they got to California—and Kurt came out in answer to Ellen's wire, Kurt and Ellen could conceal their love for each other no longer.

Ellen, believing that Beatrice would never give Kurt a divorce, and thinking that it would be better not to stay at Hollister House, decided to visit Aunt Margaret in Westchester and help her with her project of entertaining the children from the orphans' home. In doing this, she might forget her own heartache. . . . For the future seemed hopeless, until . . .

Yours, With Love

by

JEAN CAREW
Author of "First Girl," *etc.*

PRESTIGE BOOKS
NEW YORK, NEW YORK

Copyright, 1947, by Jean Carew

Prestige Books, Inc.
18 East 41st Street, New York, New York 10017

PRINTED IN THE UNITED STATES OF AMERICA

Yours, With Love

❖❖ 1 ❖❖

"Oh, it's you."

Sitting in front of her dressing table and speaking into the mirror, the orange-haired woman who was lipsticking her mouth with a lavish hand addressed the reflected image of the girl in the doorway.

"Come in," she added. "What have you been doing with yourself all day?"

"Getting a job."

The girl crossed the room as she spoke and sat down on the foot of the chaise longue. "I think I'm going to like my job, Mabilla." Her stepmother, who was thirty-six but never admitted it, liked to have the girl call her by her first name.

It seemed to minimize the difference in their ages.

Mabilla by this time had finished her lips. She picked up a comb and ran it through her startling hair. If only she had left her hair its natural color, the girl reflected, she might have found it easier to tolerate her late father's choice of a second wife. Mabilla leaned forward, her face close to the mirror. "Heavens! For a minute I thought I saw a gray hair."

She straightened up again. "A job, Ellen dear? How silly. You can put it right out of your head. I had a letter from your Aunt Margaret this morning."

"You wrote to Aunt Margaret! You know father would have forbidden you, if—if—"

"Why go into that?" Airily, "Your poor dear father always wanted to see me happy."

Ellen Marshall regarded her stepmother coldly.

"I'm going to be a private secretary—" she was beginning, but Mabilla interrupted her.

"Don't you want to hear what Aunt Maggie says?" she demanded.

Ellen, who had started to rise, sank back again.

"All right, what does she say? Not that it will make any difference in my plans."

Mabilla was rummaging in a drawer among a jumble of cosmetics.

"Where did I put that letter? It's a scream, really. Oh, here it is! Listen:

I thought I'd have you asking me to support you sooner or later. I see my dear niece Ellen did not write me, but you, who have no claim on me whatever. I've expected to hear from you since the moment I heard of poor Robert's passing. Come along, then. If you can stand me, I'll try to stand you. But remember, I'm only doing it for Robert's sake, not yours.

"The old witch!" Mabilla said. "Serves her right if we take her word for it and move in on her, Ellen. Let's both go right now and help her use up some of her money."

"You'd accept an invitation like that, after asking for charity? When you knew my father would have hated you even to hint that you thought Aunt Margaret owed us anything—which she certainly does not!"

Mabilla gave an orchid satin footstool a vicious kick.

"Why go into that? Your father was impractical, or he wouldn't have died leaving us both practically penniless." Disdaining to remember that it was she who had spent the greater part of her husband's fortune, Mabilla was flouncing about the room, switching her trailing velvet hostess gown behind her every few steps with an energetic backward kick.

"Even if Aunt Margaret really wanted us to come to live with her, I still prefer to earn my own living," Ellen said.

Mabilla came to a halt, looking at the girl with shrewd appraisal. "You've got looks. Why should you waste them on an office when you could have your Aunt Maggie eating out of your hand? After all, you are her brother's only daughter, and you could go up to that big estate and live like a human being. There must be a raft of servants with only that one old woman to wait on."

"I'm not going," said Ellen. She picked up her bag and got to her feet.

"Well, I am," Mabilla snapped at her.

Silence hung over the room for a full minute. Uneasy, Mabilla, fingering the jars of cosmetics on the glass-topped table, glanced sideways at Ellen. The girl walked to the door, opened it, then turned.

"Why don't you go to work, Mabilla?" she said.

Dull, unbecoming red slid up under the rouge on the high cheekbones, and Mabilla, suddenly rigid, seemed to have difficulty in getting her breath. Ellen took no notice.

"Are you trying to insult me?" her stepmother asked, furiously.

"Certainly not. I'm being practical. I'm not like father, you see."

Ellen waited for any further comment, but Mabilla only glared.

"It was just a suggestion. Sorry to have startled you—though it seems to me you might have thought of it yourself."

Promptly at nine-thirty the next morning, Ellen found herself in the reception room of the Feathertop Mountain Mining Company, Limited, fifteen stories above Fifth Avenue.

This was the morning she was to meet the man who would decide her future. She had dressed carefully in her good black suit, her plainest tailored blouse of white pique, and black suede pumps. It was a severe costume; the effect was "smartness with restraint," the better shops called it, she remembered. Ellen had blue-black hair, with a hint of a natural wave, and she had parted it down the middle and rolled it into a smooth chignon at the nape of her neck. Her skin had a surprisingly pale apricot tone, but her eyes were actually startling, big and wide open, of vivid blue, with such a definite fire and sparkle to them that, flashing between the silky black lashes that sprayed back from them, they had the quality of jewels. Her lips were full and the wide mouth was emphasized by the deep blue-red of her lipstick.

The manager of the employment agency had said, when Ellen applied for the job, and was given a first sharp all-over glance of appraisal, "Well now—well! You'll do!"

"I'll do for what?" asked Ellen, puzzled.

"For a special job I have here. I've interviewed over fifty girls so far; none of them fitted in. I was told just what type I must send. You're the right one!

"This job is unusual. You will have to live at the country estate of your employer, out on Long Island. He's writing a book about the mines—gold, I think he said—that he owns in the West. He gave up the presidency of the company because it was too much for his health, and I understand he's very trying to work for. Wealthy and exacting. The book's about his life as a mining engineer, and how they get gold out of mines—that kind of thing. Want to try it?"

"May I have the job?" Ellen asked, her voice level.

"I'll give you a chance to apply for it."

The woman told her to sit down for a moment while she wrote out directions. While she waited Ellen thought gratefully of the business course she had taken at the exclusive finishing school she had attended, never actually expecting to use it.

The employment manager looked up and held out a card.

"Go to this address tomorrow at nine-thirty and ask for Mr. Kurt Hollister. I'll make the appointment. Mr. Hollister is a nephew of the man you will work for if he hires you. This Mr. Kurt Hol-

YOURS, WITH LOVE

lister took over the presidency of the Feathertop Mountain Mining Company, when his uncle's health failed several years ago. You'll be on your own when you meet him, but if you click with him, he'll drive you out to the Long Island estate for an interview with his uncle. I'm not sending anyone else to see him because he told me to make a selection myself. Good luck, Miss Marshall!"

Ellen now stood hesitant just inside the door of the big reception room, trying to steady herself. The next hour or so was going to mean so very much to her!

"Yes, miss?" the receptionist inquired from her desk.

Ellen stepped forward at once.

"I have an appointment with Mr. Kurt Hollister for nine-thirty. I'm Ellen Marshall."

"Oh, yes indeed, Miss Marshall! Please go out of that door straight ahead and then it's the third door on your right." She indicated the directions with her pencil. "Just go in and wait. Mr. Hollister will be there directly."

Ellen drew in her breath sharply as she opened the door of the office to which she had been sent. In a quick glance around, her eyes caught the dull sheen of walls made of what looked like bronze and luxurious furnishings done in shades of gray. There was a massive desk down at the far end of the room against a bank of windows overlooking

Fifth Avenue. A long conference table took up almost all of one wall. It was quite impressive. Ellen crossed to the nearest chair and sat down. Through an arched doorway she glimpsed another room with walls lined with rows of beautifully bound books from floor to ceiling.

Shall I keep staring around the office, or shall I close my eyes and concentrate on what I'm going to say to Mr. Hollister? she was thinking, when the door opposite her swung open and a tall young man, very wide of shoulder, strode in.

"Good morning," he said briskly, inclining his head as he passed her on his way to the desk.

"Good morning," said Ellen, on her feet instantly.

"Be seated, please, Miss Marshall. I'll be with you in a moment."

Ellen sat down. This, of course was Mr. Kurt Hollister. She watched him open a dozen or so of the letters which lay on his desk. She looked at his blond hair, sun-bleached in streaks, and liked the contrast of it against his deeply tanned skin. She liked the firm planes of his face, that could mean only strength, yes, and courage. And the squared cleft chin—there was determination. Suddenly Ellen realized, her heart beating fast, that here was a man more interesting, more attractive than any she had ever met. He must be about thirty, but there was a boyishness about him, too.

YOURS, WITH LOVE 15

I'm staring at him! A quick sting of color in her cheeks—a quick turn of her head away from him. At that moment he looked up at her; she felt his look and turned back. He had very dark eyes, very keen. He was smiling, and there was warmth in the smile. He had laid aside the letters as he had opened them, all except one, which he had before him now, his long tanned hand beside it on the glass top of the desk. He squared his shoulders decisively, as if to get back to the business at hand, and asked, half quizzically:

"Miss Marshall, have you a nice disposition?"

Ellen was taken off guard, but only for a moment.

"Well, yes, Mr. Hollister—but I can take my own part!"

Mr. Hollister threw back his head, and white teeth flashed as his delighted laughter filled the room.

"Just wait until Paul Jean hears that answer! That's the question he asks everyone he engages for a job."

Then, at the puzzled expression in her eyes, he added hastily, "Forgive me—you didn't know, of course! Paul Jean is my uncle. You are to be his secretary, his co-worker on the book he is writing. I'm to drive you out to our place this evening so you two can meet."

"Yes, I understand," Ellen told him.

Then, as if a pleasant thought had just come to him, "Miss Marshall, I wonder if you would have time to write one letter for me right now? My own secretary is out ill."

"May I? That is, do you think I could help?" Ellen asked earnestly.

Mr. Hollister jumped up from his chair and came around to her, clasping her hand firmly.

"Come with me. We'll get a notebook and pencils from Miss Winters' office."

Ellen followed his quick strides into an office that adjoined his. Here was his secretary's desk, and chairs for people to wait. The walls were painted deep cream color, and the furniture was upholstered in cream-colored leather. What a lovely, quiet place. How could the girl work in such a room—for such a man as Mr. Hollister? Ellen picked up a notebook that was lying on top of the desk, and several pencils. She smiled up at him.

"Ready?" he asked.

They went back to his own desk and he started dictating immediately.

"Am I going too fast?" he inquired, after a few moments.

"Not at all. Don't mind me, Mr. Hollister."

Not mind her indeed, he thought, that would be impossible.

But Mr. Hollister would not have admitted, even to himself, how much aware he was of her. As he watched the lithe, slender figure and the gracefully bent dark head, he noticed how she hung on his words, looking up at him every few seconds to be sure she had his exact meaning. Her brilliant blue gaze would be intent on his own eyes for long moments, as if she were visualizing what he was saying, then back again to the notes she was taking. How pleasant it was, indeed inspiring, to have someone so interested in what he was saying. It was refreshing not to be asked to repeat what he had said, as Miss Winters had been doing so much recently. When she first started to work for him she'd been fine, but lately—yesterday, for instance, halfway through that last letter she'd stopped writing, dropped her book and pencil on the floor, and began to sob aloud, her hands pressed to her convulsed face! Horrified, Mr. Hollister had placed a hand on her heaving shoulder to quiet her, but she had flung off the hand and stumbled from the room. Thinking back, Mr. Hollister was genuinely concerned about her; she had been fiercely loyal to the company for many years. Looking now at the beautiful girl beside him, he thought, that's it! Miss Winters is getting a bit old for the fast tempo of this office. Her hair is quite gray, I've noticed. A long vacation—for her nerves.

Ellen's arresting voice brought him back with a start.

"Will that be all, Mr. Hollister?"

"Pardon me, Miss Marshall, I was thinking. Yes, that is all. Please make two carbons."

When Ellen laid the neatly typed letter before him a little later, he looked up at her with a grateful, appreciative smile. Then he read the letter through and signed it.

"If there is any other correspondence—" Ellen began, but he interrupted.

"No. You've done quite enough. You have done me a great favor."

"Not at all," Ellen answered.

"Now about driving out with me to meet my uncle. Could you be ready at four this afternoon? Will you meet me in the main lobby at the Waldorf?"

Ellen walked out of the office and went down on the elevator, filled with stirring anticipation at what lay before her! An undertow of feeling, exciting, strong, had caught her up. She wondered if Kurt Hollister felt it, too. All the way uptown she sat lightly on the seat of the taxi, leaning forward a little.

2

"Take off your hat?" Kurt Hollister invited.

Ellen stood with him beside a low, sleek roadster. As he spoke, he unlocked the car door and threw his gray felt in the back. She handed him her beret and it followed his hat.

"Get in," he said.

Ellen liked his tone of command; it suited him. He got in beside her and the car spurted ahead. She had known he would drive like this—his handling of the wheel was so effortless it looked almost like indifference.

When they left the bridge the traffic thinned out, and they streaked along the level Long Island roads. Scraps of grayed, sandy towns flashed past.

Later still, there was open country and an occasional farm, with nice, straight rows of lettuce or cabbage pointing long green fingers at them as the car whisked by. Then came the expensive part of the island, great tracts of land, fenced in.

Mansions set way back from the highway for seclusion, most likely, Ellen thought, and was about to ask whose estates some of them were when a hairpin suddenly slithered down and landed in her lap. She must have loosened it when she pulled off her beret. She retrieved it quickly with one hand, stabbed it into the curl that was falling over her shoulder, and tried to fasten it again into the knot at the back of her neck. All she succeeded in doing was to let another hairpin get away. Embarrassed, she started to catch back the tumbling black curls with both hands.

"Let it alone," said Kurt. "Better, take out all the pins. I like casual hair-dos." After a quick glance sideways at her, "Your hair is really black, isn't it?"

Ellen murmured assent, then confessed, "I only pinned it up for the job, and I wasn't very good at it. I've always worn it long."

"Just be yourself with us. Makes things easier all round."

He looked at her again after she had tucked the lustrous black hair, made curlier now by the damp sea air, back of her small ears.

"Swell!" he approved.

Very few cars passed them now. Every now and then Ellen caught the sparkle of the sea, running gold with the sunset on it. It was strange, but as they drove along she had the sensation that out here the sky was nearer to the earth than it was in the city. That's ridiculous! she chided herself. It's simply because everything is so flat and empty out here, and daylight is fading.

In spite of herself she felt a tremor of apprehension, dull and muffled, but it was there. Resolutely she fought it.

This job is a starting point for me; it is my life from now on. I must make a blank of all that has gone before, the pleasant as well as the unpleasant things; for the time being I must forget everything but my work here.

But a new doubt bobbed up: Everything before me is a blank, too. I haven't the slightest conception of what lies ahead.

Kurt Hollister's voice broke in, reassuring.

"When we come to what looks like an endless stone wall, that's Hollister House. Not such a bad ride, was it?"

"I loved it," she told him.

What she didn't tell him was that just hearing his voice had made up her mind and quieted her fears. She was now determined, come what may, to go along with this new world, the world that

Kurt Hollister lived in. She knew, above everything else, that she wanted to be near this man, at least to be near enough to see him while he went about everyday things—as now it was a delight to see the swing of his big shoulders as he turned the car into the wide drive that led to the house.

The strong smell of pine was everywhere. Dark, rigid, and important, the trees stood tall on both sides of the drive. In one of them some birds, as big as gulls, having settled for the night, resented the oncoming car, and flapped wide wings angrily while they screamed hoarse insults at the intruders.

Around one final curve, and they were racing for a huge, solemn, solid structure of stone, built on a natural foundation of rock jutting out in a triangle into the water.

It's a castle out of the middle ages, and it's throwing itself into the sea, was Ellen's fleeting impression, as the car stopped and a liveried servant ran down to meet them.

"Here we are, Miss Marshall. Come along."

Kurt was out of the car and bounding up the steps, so Ellen did some fast stepping herself and sprinted right along after him. She felt an absurd urge to grab hold of his coat; he seemed to be outdistancing her with his long strides. It would never do to lose him in this untried vastness.

Kurt had taken only a step into the great hall,

YOURS, WITH LOVE 23

Ellen a close two feet behind him, when the air was rent with loud wails and the anguished squealing of reluctant brakes from the drive. Kurt's car was gone, Ellen knew; she had seen it driven off by the servant. They turned back to see a battered red and yellow taxi lurching toward the house. A girl, head and shoulders out of the window, long blond hair flying, waved wildly in their direction. Tears streamed down the white face, and the owner was yelling at the top of a fine pair of lungs.

"Wait! Oh, Kurt—wait!"

With assorted sound effects the taxi stopped dead at the steps, the door burst open, suitcases dumped out. Kurt raced down and the hysterical girl threw herself with a flying leap into his outflung arms. The man took the impact without a quiver.

What timing, Ellen thought, like a scene in a ballet.

The girl looked very young, perhaps seventeen —and the brokenhearted weeping went right on. Kurt, his arm around her slender shoulders, was leading her into the house.

"This is my Cousin Flossie, Miss Marshall," he said in an aside to Ellen.

Ellen was about to speak, but the girl didn't even turn her head in her direction. Kurt had told her a little about Flossie on the way out.

"She is the only sister I have," he had said.

"We've all spoiled her outrageously, but she's such a lovable wench. We grew up together—although I'm older—here at Hollister House."

No one was paying the least attention to her, so Ellen went on in by herself and stood to one side. She could hear hurrying feet in different parts of the enormous house, getting people to the front hall at their best speed. A white-capped maid skimmed down the curved central staircase; the butler, with dignified tread, arrived at almost the same moment. Ellen became conscious of the sound, drawing nearer, of the thump of a heavy walking stick hitting the hardwood floor. Then there came a smart smack on the swing door directly in back of her. Instinctively, Ellen spun about and saw the silver head of a heavy cane come poking through the door, in the vigorous grasp of a majestic and handsome white-haired woman.

"Out of my way, young woman." The silver-headed cane came down smartly, although it didn't hit hard enough to hurt, on first one, then the other, of Ellen's black suede pump toes, which she hastily drew out of reach.

"Out of my way, I say," the dramatic, rich voice filled the great hall imperiously. The woman swept past Ellen on her way over to Kurt, who was still trying to quiet Flossie.

"Save me, Kurt—save me from that brute I married," wailed Flossie.

YOURS, WITH LOVE 25

Maybe that queenly one will give her attention to someone else now, gratefully reflected Ellen as she regarded the stately back moving stiffly away from her. Her relief was short-lived, however, for the next instant the woman remembered that she had never before laid eyes on Ellen. She about-faced and came back, leveling a long-handled lorgnette straight at the girl.

"Who are you?" she inquired haughtily. "Speak up, speak up! Who are you, and what are you doing here at Hollister House?"

At her approach Ellen had judiciously slid her feet under a small table nearby; but the precaution didn't work, for the silver-headed cane flicked at her wrist instead, as the older woman rapped out her questions. Kurt came to the rescue, calling from across the hall.

"Aunt Olivette, this is Miss Marshall, Uncle Paul Jean's new secretary. My Aunt Olivette, Miss Marshall."

Aunt Olivette acknowledged the introduction by a long, piercing stare through the glasses.

"All right, all right, Marshall. Why doesn't somebody tell me things?"

With a wave of the cane toward the maid, she ordered, "Hilda, take Marshall up to the west wing sea room at once."

Then she turned to Flossie.

"Stop that infernal bawling this minute, Flossie

—you make my head ache. You've upset me and the whole house. Stop it, I say!"

She whirled on Ellen again. "Dinner is at eight, Marshall. See you're on time."

Again the cane flicked snappily across the back of Ellen's brief wool skirt, as she was about to follow the maid. She turned on Aunt Olivette and the blue eyes flamed sapphire into the sharp old ones. Aunt Olivette smiled, and she spoke with high good humour.

"You've got spunk, Marshall. I like that, but don't mind my cane—they're only love taps."

The wide corridor on the second floor had splendid crystal chandeliers spaced at regular intervals, and although it wasn't really dark yet, these were lighted, throwing out a glory of prismatic colors in all directions. Just as Ellen reached the top of the stairs, a woman's voice, raised in song, filled the house. Ellen gripped the railing and stood spellbound as the clear, flutelike soprano lilted up the stair-well:

"One day when we were young,
One wonderful morning in May,
You told me you loved me,
When we were young one day."

Strauss, Ellen thought. How father loved his music. He'd sit and listen while I played it—fire dancing on the logs in the fireplace. Resolutely she dismissed the memory. The maid waited for her down the hall.

"What a wonderful voice," Ellen said.

"Miss Olivette. When she gets upset she sings and plays. Miss Flossie upset her. Says singing takes her out of this wicked world." She added, "It is grand, her singing. She was a concert singer in years gone by."

"So that's it," Ellen exclaimed. "That's why she makes me think of long, white kid gloves, flowers, excitement, crowds. She's beautiful still. No wonder she has an air about her."

The maid held a door open. As Ellen stepped over the threshold she caught her breath sharply. The entire wall of the room looking out over the ocean was made of glass, the center part a door that led out to a balcony; floor-length windows on either side swung back into the room when open. She went out on the balcony, and stood there, spellbound. It was like being on the deck of an ocean liner. Night was coming on, and the horizon was blurred, but far out from the rocky promontory on which the house was built, she could see heavy waves knifing across the expanse of dark green water. They rose ponderously to a great height, with a sound like distant thunder, then hurled themselves furiously at the beach and rocks below.

The maid spoke at Ellen's elbow.

"May I unpack for you, Miss?"

"Thank you, no. I'll manage."

The maid busied herself with opening doors, fastening windows, and other small tasks. Just for something to say, Ellen asked:

"Will she be all right? The girl downstairs, I mean—Miss Flossie."

"Oh, that Miss Flossie, with her carryin' on." She brushed the situation away with a flip of her hand. "She's just married, six months past, that is. And she's back here screamin' and goin' on two and three times a month ever since. Them and their night clubs and their parties; they're just plain spoiled. That's what ails them both—too much money, and young and headstrong."

Heeding Aunt Olivette's warning not to be late for dinner, Ellen started down at a quarter to eight. Her foot had no sooner reached the bottom step than the cane began a lively tattoo, evidently meant to attract her attention. She followed the sound to an open door and found Aunt Olivette standing in the middle of a softly lighted room. The old lady leaned on her cane and frankly looked the girl over with sharp eyes. Ellen returned the direct gaze, deeply interested in this unusual woman. She couldn't even make a guess about her age; it might be sixty—or seventy. With Aunt Olivette it couldn't possibly matter how old she was. Ellen was fascinated by the long, slender feet, in very expensive-looking shoes; the exquisite gown of white silk jersey, soft and clinging. She had long-fingered, aristocratic hands, both of them laden with diamonds.

"So you're going to work with Paul Jean. Well —well. You're quite beautiful, you know; you carry yourself well. Paul Jean can't abide awkward women." Then, half to herself, and with a sparkle of malicious mirth in her glance, she murmured, "Wonder how Beatrice is going to like having you about the house." She went over to one of the fireside settees.

"We must have a talk, you and I. Paul Jean may not get in for dinner. He's out fiddling with that boat of his. If he doesn't arrive, come to my sitting room after we've finished."

"She'll pay you no visit tonight, Olivette. This young lady wants a good night's sleep, so we can start with a bang on my book tomorrow."

Striding toward them came a refreshing giant of a man, middle-aged, a dash of gray in his thick brown hair. He bent and landed a light kiss on Olivette's cheek. He was deeply tanned and wore a white linen suit and a bright pink shirt, open at the bronzed throat—clearly a law unto himself in the matter of attire. He held out his hand to Ellen.

"You're Miss Marshall, of course. Kurt said he would bring you out tonight."

His handshake was vigorous. He looked sharply

at her for several minutes, in absolute silence. Seeming to like what he saw, his big, jovial voice boomed out again:

"So you're going to help me write a book?"

"May I try, Mr. Hollister?"

"Indeed you may. We'll start tomorrow morning."

A high, clear, altogether lovely voice broke in:

"Hi! Everybody! I'm here, waiting for welcome-home kisses." It was Flossie, just inside the door, arms flung out toward them, her beautiful red mouth in an exaggerated pucker ready to be kissed. But the next moment she floated past, straight into the arms of Paul Jean.

"Uncle Paul Jean—you darling."

Next Flossie brushed the older woman's hair with her lips. "Dearest Olivette," she cooed.

There wasn't the trace of a tear on that flawless complexion; not a sign of red-rimmed eyes.

Ellen's glance caught Kurt's as he came into the room. He came directly over to her.

"We must apologize for the reception you got this evening," he said. "Flossie is very high-strung, but she's quite recovered, you see."

There could be no doubt of his affection for his cousin. He was watching her with absolute approval as she lit a cigarette gracefully, and then perched on the arm of Paul Jean's chair, her arm around his neck. Certainly the girl made an extremely light-hearted picture as she sat swinging one small sandaled foot back and forth with a great deal of spirit, causing the blue chiffon of her dinner gown to circle wildly in frothy swirls. Her pale gold hair was combed straight back from her forehead and nearly reached her waist in the back. Suddenly, noticing Kurt standing talking to Ellen, she hopped off the chair arm and came over to them with a little running step. Kurt introduced them.

The two girls were the same height. Each looked for a moment straight into the eyes of the other, unsmiling. Then Flossie said sweetly:

"Oh, how super—you type and everything? And will you be a dear and help me with my old budget? Paul Jean's mean to me. Makes me figure up what I spend."

Making no pretense of waiting for Ellen's answer, with another little rush she was off again, back to Paul Jean, to cling to his arm as he got up and included everybody with a sweeping gesture.

"Is this all there is of my damn family for dinner tonight?" he demanded loudly. "And where's that sea dog of a Jeffers? I'm starved. *Jeffers!*"

Jeffers, it turned out, was the butler, and he made his appearance at that very moment to announce dinner.

"Mount and ride, girls and boys." Paul Jean shooed them toward the arched doorway. He caught up to Ellen and walked beside her.

"Pay me no mind, Miss Marshall. I'm really an old fool when it comes to my family. Love 'em all, want them around me. Cover up my feelings by being rude."

But that wasn't all of his family for dinner that night. Even as he spoke Ellen saw his expression change surprisingly. It became set and severe as he stopped and waited for two people who had come into the room. Ellen saw an extravagantly tall, extravagantly handsome, dark young man in evening clothes, striding forward. A tall, straight-up-and-down figure of a woman walked beside him, her hand in the crook of his arm. She was dressed in gray. Her hair was an indefinite brown, with no sheen, and her eyes were the same color, and lusterless; even her skin had a gray overtone. A faint, mirthless smile appeared fixed on the straight mouth. Kurt hurried over to them and spoke to the woman.

"Why, Beatrice, you told me you wouldn't be able to come down."

He attempted to take her hand, but she snapped it away peevishly.

"You never know what I will do—do you?"

It was a sharp, high voice, very disagreeable. Ellen felt instantly repelled and chilled.

"What brings you back so soon, Clyde?" Kurt asked the man.

"Such a warm welcome, dear cousin. It's been three months I've been away. Don't tell me you didn't miss me." The man laughed lightly, an infectious laugh.

When Kurt made no answer he went over to Paul Jean.

"Maybe you're glad to see me, Uncle. I flew in this afternoon. May I have my old job back once more? Tell the honest truth—you never could replace me as manager of your estate, now could you?"

Ellen, looking at him, thought that the pagan gods must have looked like this man. But why did everyone treat him as if he were the bearer of bad news? So far, no one had even spoke to him, except Kurt, and his few words could scarcely be construed as cordial. Paul Jean broke what was becoming a silence.

"Every time I set eyes on you, Clyde, sure as shootin' it means trouble for me. You go out of your way to dig it up. Last time you left it was to grow oranges on an island. What happened to that? Authorities after you?"

"Take it easy, Uncle. There's no price on my head. Simply too many oranges. Got monotonous. I sold out—made money on the deal. Do I get the job? Am I your new estate manager?"

"All right, take over. Matter of fact, I'm glad to have you, come to think of it. Give me more time for doing my book. This is Miss Marshall, my secretary, going to help me with the job." He said to Ellen, "This is my nephew, Clyde Hollister."

There was still one of the company to be accounted for—Beatrice. Kurt began to speak. Just a few words, but they blotted out for Ellen everything in the world, so that for a few seconds she neither heard nor saw anything else that went on in the room. Then she was conscious of Aunt Olivette's voice, magnetic, compelling:

"Marshall, doesn't dinner interest you?"

Ellen realized that she had lagged behind the others, and that Aunt Olivette was standing waiting for her. Mechanically she moved to her side and walked with her toward the dining room. But still those words of Kurt's echoed and re-echoed in her ears.

Kurt had stood, curiously wooden, looking neither at Beatrice nor Ellen as he spoke.

It's not true—it's not true. Ellen felt herself denying what she had heard, was vaguely surprised to find she had not spoken aloud, as she crossed the great hall with Aunt Olivette.

That cold-eyed woman, that gray shadow hanging on Clyde's arm, looking up at him—"Beatrice," Kurt had said, "Miss Marshall, Paul Jean's new secretary. Miss Marshall, this is my wife."

Far away, among the green hills of Westchester,

YOURS, WITH LOVE

a vaguely astonished Mabilla was turning down her narrow bed, preparatory to what she hoped would be a good night's rest.

"And boy, do I need it!" she sighed.

Mabilla had been astonished so repeatedly since arriving at Aunt Margaret's that she had settled down by now, several hours later, into a mild and continuous state of surprise. Nothing was as she had expected it to be, but by the end of the day she had grown so accustomed to being astonished that she was hardly conscious of any emotional jolt, no matter how unexpected were the fresh revelations of life on a suburban estate which confronted her at every turn.

At this moment she was wondering, without any very lively curiosity, if that strange moaning sound she could faintly hear was some human creature in distress somewhere out on the lawn beneath her windows, or whether it came from the dovecotes built along the stable eaves.

For Mabilla's room was in the stable. So indeed was Aunt Margaret's and that of old Hetty, Aunt Margaret's personal maid and companion of a lifetime.

There were other servants, living in the house itself, and in a couple of small cottages hidden in the masses of shrubbery. The house was huge, ornate in the 1890 manner, adorned with wooden lace and crowned with cupolas. Mabilla had eyed it with pleased interest as her taxi rolled up the driveway on that first day. It was just a hack she had hired at the station, but Mabilla, leaning back on the cushion, had had a distinct sensation of entering a world to which she by nature belonged. An opulent world, where even the roofs on the house she was to occupy were redundant.

And then the taxi rolled on past the front door, a screen door, through which Mabilla could see, in one fleeting glance, clear through to another open doorway at the back of the house, framing a garden. She would have shouted to the taxi driver, where was he going, for the love of Pete, except that, just at that moment, a baseball sailed past her nose, through one open window of the cab and out the other. A wild yell followed the ball, and Mabilla became aware of a round, freckled boy's face, apparently hung on an evergreen tree, like a toy on a Christmas tree. The taxi driver, unaware of either the narrow escape of his passenger, or the odd visage wreathed in green, now put on speed and whisked briskly around a turn in the drive.

Instantly the ball became a minor incident. For behind the screening evergreens the lawn was teeming with children. Close to the tall hedge a baseball diamond had been laid out, and here a team of small boys was hard at practice. A yelling mob of younger boys and girls was playing in the center of the playground, while other children swarmed like monkeys over gymnasium equipment, hung over the edge of a miniature pool, and swung dizzily through the air on a half-dozen swings.

So confused by this scene was Mabilla that she did not even protest when the taxi driver pulled up in front of what was easily recognizable as the stable, and said, "Here y'are, lady." Flurried and astonished, she hunted for money in her handbag, and after the man was gone, lifted the knocker of the stable door.

A stout, elderly, but undeniably competent-looking woman in slacks, a smock, and a wide-brimmed, straw gardening hat opened the door. Mabilla said, uncertaintly, "Is Aunt M— I mean, is Mrs. Sloane—" She got no further.

"Come in, come in," said the woman briskly. "You're Mabilla, Bob's second wife. He sent me your picture. Where's Ellen?"

"Ellen wouldn't come," said Mabilla, in an aggrieved tone. "She got a job in some office."

"Good for her," said the woman, now identified by Mabilla, with a sinking heart, as Aunt Margaret. She led the way into the kitchen—of all places! "That's the kind of spirit I like to see in a young 'un," Aunt Margaret said. "Ellen must take after the Marshall side of the family. None of us Marshalls ever asked anybody for favors."

Mabilla, not quite sure whether or not this was

intended as a reflection upon herself, decided to say something general and soothing.

"Well, it takes all kinds to make a world," she murmured, with forced cheeriness.

"Unfortunately!" snapped Aunt Margaret. "I suppose you're hungry? Make yourself a cheese sandwich, or fry an egg, if you like—they're in the icebox. I've got to see to the children."

"Thanks," said Mabilla.

"You saw some of the children as you came in, didn't you?" Aunt Margaret went on. "They're sent out every day from the city—from settlement houses and orphanages, different ones in turn. I've turned over the big house and the grounds to them."

"Do they come here every day?" Mabilla could not conceal her sharp dismay.

"Every day but Sunday," said Aunt Margaret. "Get yourself a snack and come on out and help. There's enough work for more than a dozen women."

From the moment, a half-hour later, that she stepped out on the lawn, in search of Aunt Margaret, until she was getting ready to drop exhausted into bed, Mabilla had had no time to consider her position. And now that she had the time, she found she couldn't keep her eyes open. She decided to forget, for once, the elaborate beauty ritual with which she always prepared for bed. She didn't even bother to cold cream her face. As for problems—I'll worry about what next tomorrow, was her last waking thought. That is, if I have the time.

❖❖ 3 ❖❖

Ellen arrived in the breakfast room at eight-thirty, to find Paul Jean already there. He was drinking coffee. Overflowing manila files were stacked on the table on each side of him.

"Might be easier to reconstruct a bombed city, you're thinking, are you, from the looks of these notes?" he asked Ellen.

"Oh, no, Mr. Hollister."

"This 'mess' here is my original material—notes left by my grandfather, who got the mines going when he was a young man. Damned good stuff."

After breakfast, he said they'd work in the garden. He led the way across a double terrace, down a flight of wooden steps, built over the rocks, to an exotic garden, a few feet below the level of the lawn that stretched away from the house at this side. They walked among flowering hedges and trees full of pink blossoms that Ellen didn't recognize. She said so.

"Those trees? English hawthorn, I think Clyde said they were. Clyde is responsible for all the landscaping, and it's damned good. Got to give the devil his due; when he applies himself he can't be beat."

"They look like flying wedding cakes," Ellen ventured.

But it wasn't Clyde she wanted to hear about. She had lingered over her grapefruit and coffee to the last excusable minute, in the hope that Kurt would appear. She simply could not put out of her mind his strange manner and the way he had looked when he introduced his wife, Beatrice. Ellen couldn't forget her, either. All through dinner the woman had dawdled over her food, not eating anything that Ellen could see. The girl couldn't help looking at her, for her insolent gaze seemed to draw her own eyes to hers against Ellen's will. It was plain that Beatrice resented the newcomer; she didn't speak to anyone during the meal, except once to Kurt.

"You didn't want me to come down to dinner tonight, did you?" she said.

"Why do you say that?" Kurt asked, and again

there was that unyielding look about him, and his tone was icy.

But Beatrice did not answer. Her eyes had thick, heavy-looking lids, and she lowered them then, as if she wanted to get away from the sight of him.

Mr. Hollister had dictated almost steadily until eleven o'clock. He stopped to light his pipe.

"How about you, Miss Marshall? Cigarette?"

Ellen did want a smoke, and he lit a cigarette for her. He tamped his pipe and walked about.

"Get up and stretch your legs a bit, Miss Marshall. We mustn't go at this writing too hard. Let's walk down to the pond."

Ellen was glad to walk a little. They went through a wooded section, beautifully laid out—Clyde's work again, of course; and then below lay the pond, as Mr. Hollister called it. But it was a large artificial lake, really, circular, with flagstones making a border all around.

"Such blue water," Ellen exclaimed. "Turquoise."

"The basin is painted blue," said Mr. Hollister. "It's good-looking, that spot of blue water among the trees."

On the way back Ellen couldn't resist asking, "Has Mr. Kurt Hollister gone in to town this morning?"

"Oh, sure. Gets an early start every morning, before eight usually, to avoid the traffic." Then, as a thought struck him, "Oh, I say now, that's too bad. Did you want him to bring something back for you?"

"Nothing like that. Oh, no." Ellen suddenly felt at a loss to explain why she had asked for Kurt. "I wanted to thank him for bringing me out—it was a lovely drive. I didn't get a chance to tell him last night," she struggled with the words. She should never have asked.

But his hearty voice fell gratefully on her ears.

"Don't you worry your head about things like that. Kurt was glad to drive you out."

Her agitation was dying away when they came within sight of their chairs and the table with her notebook on it. Standing there and flipping over the pages of the notebook was Beatrice. She had on a black dress today, and in daylight Ellen saw that the woman herself, her skin and hair, looked more lifeless than ever. In her very drabness, however, Ellen sensed a hidden force lurking. And that almost imperceptible smile was there, fixed on the thin lips. Beatrice didn't speak when she looked up and saw them coming.

"Do my eyes deceive me, Beatrice? You in the garden?" Paul Jean roared out. "You always said it was damp, gave you neuritis or headaches or something."

This burst of greeting accomplished, Paul Jean drew up his chair for her.

"Sit down, Beatrice, sit down. Not for long though. We're hell-bent for leather with the book. Got to put a sign up 'Authors at Work.' "

"I won't sit down at all."

The woman slapped the notebook back on the table, so that the pages sprawled open and it hit the neat row of sharpened pencils Ellen had lined up. They started to roll off, and in spite of the leap Paul Jean made to stop them, they fell on the grass. Without a word of apology, Beatrice said sharply:

"It's about your meals, Miss Marshall. No doubt you felt quite out of place last night at dinner, among people who are strangers to you. I've arranged for you to take your meals with Mrs. Hobbs, our housekeeper, hereafter. I should think Kurt might have told you that last night."

So saying, she turned her back on them both. Paul Jean looked explosive at first; then he stood erect, with almost the same set look of restraint Ellen had seen on Kurt's face when he made the introduction last night. His voice was controlled as he called:

"Come back here for a moment, Beatrice."

Beatrice came back. Men in the gold mines had been known to obey without question when they heard that note in Paul Jean's voice.

"Now listen carefully to me. No one in this house is to tell Miss Marshall what to do—except me. After only a few hours of work with her this morning I already feel I couldn't do without her. I want her with us for meals; if I go to New York, I want her along—even if I have to go west later for particular records at the mines, she's to go with me. I want her to become used to me, my moods, my ways of expressing myself. I know she will be invaluable to me."

Beatrice simply stood, facing them, but staring out into space. Paul Jean spoke again, his voice sharper.

"You understand?"

"I have excellent hearing," Beatrice answered insolently, and left.

"My word, but she's exasperating. Something wrong with her nerves, Miss Marshall. She's been like that for quite a few years. She and Kurt were married eight years ago. They knew each other as children. Her parents' estate is next to ours."

"Does she suffer?" Ellen asked.

"Hell, no. Excuse me, Miss Marshall. I'll have to mind my language. It's nerves, they say. It surprised me so to see her out here. She stays in her own rooms for weeks at a time, even months." Then almost to himself, "Not alone, either, is my guess."

"She must be very unhappy," Ellen said. Then,

her voice low, "Mr. Hollister must be unhappy, too."

"And me." Paul Jean sprang up with the words and took a turn about the garden, then back.

"Kurt is like my son. Now, where were we?"

Ellen read the last sentence and he began once more to dictate, but his voice was husky.

"That would be quite all right, Mr. Hollister," Ellen interrupted, "to take my meals with the housekeeper. I'm terribly sorry this happened."

"Nonsense! See here, Ellen Marshall, you going to tell me what to do, too? By the way, I like that, name, Ellen. Save a lot of time if I call you that. Do you mind?"

"Of course I don't mind. I'd like it."

"Now let's put wheels under this story, Ellen," he shouted in great good humor, and started at his papers again with a big flourish.

"Yes, here we are. Grandfather is going to build a log cabin. Put this down:

" 'Shelter was indispensable. My partner was in such a hurry to make a fortune that he wouldn't help me, and off he tramped with a pick over his shoulder and a knife thrust in his belt. I got myself four poles and—' "

Right at that point the lilting voice of Aunt Olivette fell upon the flowers and the trees and the ears of Paul Jean and Ellen. Moreover, Aunt Olivette's voice didn't alone fall on the ear—it penetrated. But it was lovely. They could see her, now, walking down the wooden stairs and starting along the path toward them. She was in white again, cane in one hand, and in the other the streamers of an immense white garden hat that she was looping around and around, keeping time to:

"*There'll come a time, there'll come a time . . .*"

Ellen didn't know all the words herself, but it was Strauss again.

"*Looking at you and wanting you so,
Knowing you want me, too.*"

She had not finished the verse when she got up to them, so she planted herself squarely in front of them and, with a few final rounds of the hat, finished it.

Paul Jean was totally unappreciative, or he made believe he was. Secretly, Ellen could see how proud he was of this sister and her singing.

"Just heaven!" he shouted. "We're working, can't you see? Must you stage a concert in the middle of my first chapter? Just when I was talking so well, too."

"I'm not going to let you starve your beautiful secretary, book or not. Both of you get into the house and fresh up. Then get back here. It's lunchtime and I'm going to have it with you, out here in this gorgeous air."

When Ellen got back, a table had been set under

the trees, and Clyde was there. He had on white riding breeches and shirt. His riding boots shone like mirrors. A brilliant red, yellow, and purple scarf was knotted loosely, ascot fashion, around his throat. He came at once to Ellen.

He took her hand in his, as if it were the most natural thing in the world to do, and led her to a place at the table beside Aunt Olivette. And he kept right on talking to Paul Jean.

"Could you possibly spare a morning, sometime soon, to ride out with me, Uncle? The horses and cows are really in fine shape, but I'd still like to make the improvements in the stables and the sheds to lessen the fire hazards that I spoke about before."

"You have those plans drawn up somewhere about, haven't you, Clyde? Go along without me. I remember most of it. I trust your judgment. I'm really going strong on my book."

"Tomorrow is Sunday. You won't work all day on Sunday, will you? In the afternoon, say. Bring Miss Marshall along. Would you like to ride over the estate, Miss Marshall?"

There was a dead pause as Ellen looked toward Paul Jean for approval, but Aunt Olivette said:

"Of course, Marshall wants to see the estate and the animals. Do you want her to think we're heathens, working on the Sabbath?"

Paul Jean, starting to protest, rested one elbow on the table, causing it to tip perilously, but Aunt Olivette waved her napkin commandingly at him.

"And I'll ride out with you as far as the stables," she supplemented. "I haven't seen the horses in I don't know when."

"But my book, only just begun. The beginning is so important." Paul Jean slapped his napkin up and down on the table to emphasize his words.

"Don't you allow Paul Jean to turn you into one of those 'take-a-note-take-a-note-take-a-note' secretaries, Marshall," said Aunt Olivette, "so that you'll have to grope around the house with work-blind eyes."

They were laughing at the tragedy she had impishly got into her words, so Paul Jean subsided.

"We'll ride over the estate Sunday afternoon," he said with highly colored submission. "We'll ride and we'll ride. We'll then change horses and ride some more—we'll ride in relays."

But everyone was laughing so now at his wild picture of them that he joined in.

Clyde leaned close to Ellen. "Paul Jean has good blood lines here. Wait and see. We'll get a good horse for you to ride."

He got up from the table abruptly, excused himself, and went away to his business. In a few moments Aunt Olivette went back to the house, to get a beauty nap, she said. The dictating was resumed. Words came to Paul Jean easily, or perhaps it was love of his subject, for in his very tones Ellen felt the deep affection he had for these forebears of his. He wanted to put down the things his grandfather and his father had done, for people to read; he thought they were wonderful, and, as the story unfolded, Ellen thought so, too.

"Let's call it a day, Ellen," he suddenly burst out. "I'm not used to doing one thing for so long at a time. Will you get my papers together and take them into the library? You'll see a big desk open there. Put them in and lock it, and you keep the key. I'll go down to the boat for a while."

He was gone. Ellen was alone; papers were everywhere, on the table beside her, on the grass, with weights on them. Paul Jean had called for another long table and they were spread all over that. Her hand was cramped from the continuous writing, and her eyes were tired. She closed them. She didn't know how long she sat there. Perfume from unnumbered flowers poured in upon her; birds sang madly—and sang on, and on. . . .

"Intruding?"

A voice with a buoyant note sent excitement whipping through Ellen's consciousness. She couldn't move for the realization that she knew the voice—Kurt's. He was there, speaking to her. She opened her eyes slowly, until they were wide, regarding him.

"The blackest hair and the bluest eyes. The sky itself isn't bluer." He was standing a little way off, looking at her as he would at an oil painting.

"Pardon my saying that, Miss Marshall, but it is such an unusual combination. Out here in the daylight it is striking.

He threw himself down on the smooth grass.

"This is refreshing." He breathed in deeply. "Those petunias are something, aren't they? That perfume gets heavier as the sun goes down. Did you know that?"

"No," Ellen said.

"Aunt Olivette told me. She knows everything about flowers—lives for 'em. By the way, where's the writer of books?" He turned over, propped his square chin on a brown hand so he could see her better.

"Oh, we worked nearly all day," Ellen replied, her voice sounding cold in her effort to remain calm.

At this moment, absurdly, she could see him as a little boy romping in this very garden, with bare brown legs and hair bright as the sun, tousled and damp from play. He looked so like a boy now, looking up at her, his mouth solemn but his eyes merry.

With a business-like bustle, she sprang up and began scrambling the papers together. She was dismayed at her thoughts.

"Here, let me help you," Kurt said. "There's no rush. We've got until dinnertime, haven't we?"

Ellen forced her hands to steadiness and, together, they got the papers into neat piles, then into the manila folders.

"You're home early?" she asked.

"The office is not open at all on Saturday. I had some loose ends to take care of and an appointment with a man from the West, superintendent of the mines."

They walked back through the garden and up the wooden stairs over the rocks, across the terraces and into the house. Kurt carried the files.

"I'll put these away in Paul Jean's desk. Rest a little before dinner, why don't you? I'm going for a swim."

He did not ask her to join him. She wished he had. She didn't feel one bit tired—not since he had got home. But she would see him at dinner.

Ellen took a shower and lay down and closed her eyes. But the next minute she was up, dashing for the closet and inspecting her wardrobe. Her trunk had arrived, and one of the maids had unpacked it. She decided on a white blouse with crystal embroidery, and the white gabardine skirt of a suit.

She went back to the bed and forced herself to lie still for a little while. Her skin burned slightly from the all-day exposure to the sun, but when she was finally dressed she noticed it looked very nice against the white of her blouse.

When she got downstairs Clyde was there, in a white dinner jacket and dark trousers. He looked handsome, very sure of himself. He was smoking a cigarette when Ellen came in, an elbow on the white marble mantel. He watched her as she came halfway across the room. He smiled at her, and she had a feeling that this smile was especially for her. Her face glowed under the scrutiny. Clyde went to the radio and turned it on. A throbbing rumba.

Holding out his arms, Clyde came to her. They danced. As she knew he would be, Clyde was the best dancer she had ever danced with.

"Angel," he said once, softly.

Ellen felt, if he was calling her that, she should rebuke him, in some way. However, she didn't have to say anything, for Aunt Olivette, Paul Jean, and Jeffers all appeared right then and they went in to dinner, after Jeffers had reported Flossie was dining with friends.

Beatrice wasn't there; Kurt wasn't there. Before the first course a maid came in and silently removed two plates and the silver that went with them. No one said anything about it. That was that, it seemed.

Clyde was amusing and interesting. He kept Paul Jean and Aunt Olivette laughing about the goings-on of the natives on the island where he'd been growing oranges. He was droll and some of the things he related were a bit improper, but very gay.

They went to the music room after dinner and Clyde played and sang, in a fine baritone, ballads with Aunt Olivette. They did some opera, too. They sang in French, Italian, and Spanish. Clyde had so many accomplishments and he displayed them generously.

When she felt sure Kurt would not appear, Ellen begged to be excused. The question that had edged everything else out of her mind—where was Kurt?—all through the evening, could not be asked. That she didn't know where Beatrice was either was not important, she thought. But she was wrong.

Kurt was having dinner that evening in the apartment of his wife, and by his wife's request. Ellen was to learn later that all of these people had separate and private living quarters here in the mansion. Beatrice had a duplex apartment, and she stayed in it most of the time. You couldn't just go to Beatrice's apartment, you had to wait until you had an invitation—her husband, Kurt, just the same as anyone else.

Kurt had been surprised to receive his wife's message that she wanted him to have dinner with her. It had been several weeks since he had been asked. He didn't want to have dinner with her tonight, although it never occurred to him to tell her so.

He went slowly up the private stairway to his wife's apartment and rang the bell. Beatrice opened the door. For a moment Kurt stood there in astonishment. Beatrice was dressed in soft yellow, which took away some of the drabness of her coloring, and there was a yellow rose at the vee of her bodice. She hadn't worn anything but black or gray for several years. She had put something on her hair to make it shine, and she had on a tinge of lipstick.

She smiled faintly and said, "Come in."

He stepped in, and looking at her unbelievingly, said pleasantly, "Expecting company?"

She clasped her hands loosely in front of her and her head bent forward on the long scrawny neck, so that he could only see her averted face.

"Why?" she asked, coldly.

"I meant, aren't you dressed for company?"

"Other women dress for my husband. I dressed for you."

The sting was back in her voice. Kurt was puzzled and looked it. He tried desperately to retrieve himself.

"How charming you look," he began. But he found himself addressing her long, thin back, encased in the new yellow gown. She sat down at the table without saying anything else to him, so all he could do was follow. She rang a bell and a maid brought in the fruit cup. The expression on Beatrice's face was so unpleasant that Kurt looked the other way.

"I suppose you think it's a waste of time to look at your own wife. It's much pleasanter to look at some one new?" she inquired in a flat, conversational tone.

Kurt sat dumbfounded. Through all the disagreeableness and bitter dying of his hopes in the last few years, Beatrice had never once said anything of that nature. He spread out his hands on the exquisite lace of the tablecloth in a gesture of absolute futility. Beatrice rang for the maid. Something was wrong with the table setting. Kurt vaguely realized that a salad fork or something of the sort was missing. The scolding was terrific.

From there on, the dinner followed the pattern of many previous dinners of late years. The meat was always overdone, or it was underdone. Sharp reprimands filled the air. A quiet word of explanation to the servant would have been more efficient. Beatrice could work herself up into a frenzy of fault-finding that would last right up until the end of the meal. She didn't know what effect these dreadful complaints had on Kurt, or she didn't care. The unfortunate maid was accustomed to the noisy lectures and usually took them in her stride, but tonight for some reason they made her nervous, too. As she was at last pouring the coffee, her hand shook and she spilled some on the lace tablecloth, with quite a few spatters on the yellow gown as well.

Beatrice sprang up.

"Get out," she ordered, "both of you! Send Mrs. Hobbs up to me." She ran to her bedroom and slammed the door shut violently. They could both hear sobbing, broken, breathless, horrible sobbing.

Kurt told the maid he was sorry and gave her a five-dollar bill.

"Buy yourself something," he said. Without looking at the girl again, who was crying, too, he said, "I'm sorry."

From his own rooms he called the physician who was in regular attendance on Beatrice. It was a routine call. The doctor was required two or three times every week for treatment of one mood or another.

❖❖ 4 ❖❖

Sunday was a glorious summer day. Kurt, shaken by last night's senseless outburst from Beatrice, found it hard to settle down to anything. He tried to read in his own rooms, found himself, instead of concentrating on the page, saying over and over, "If only something could be done for her."

His rooms looked down on the terrace, and finally, hearing the sound of gay talk below, he went to the open window.

"What's going on?" he called down.

Clyde and Ellen stepped out where he could see them, then Aunt Olivette and Paul Jean.

"We're riding out to see the horses," Paul Jean shouted back at him. "Get down here, man, and join us. Do you good."

"Right you are," Kurt yelled. "Wait for me."

He felt that a brisk ride on a good horse was just what he needed.

They all rode out to the stables in the station wagon. Ellen sat beside Kurt on the front seat, for he held out his hand to her as soon as he slid behind the wheel. They were all in riding clothes, Ellen, giving thanks that her trunk had arrived, wearing jodhpurs and a white riding coat.

When they got to the north pasture, it was Clyde who sprang out of the car and around to open the door for Ellen; and that was at the very same moment that Kurt reached across her for the door handle.

"Sorry, old boy," Clyde said with an air of agreeable deviltry, Ellen thought. Then, catching sight of Kurt's face, she decided it wasn't so agreeable. Could it be that these two men had a fixed dislike, or something deeper, for each other? She recalled that Clyde had not seemed exactly pleased when Kurt had taken the driver's seat and asked her to sit beside him. Clyde had scarcely spoken a word all the way out.

A brace of ecstatic great Danes bore down upon them the minute the car stopped. There was a groom in full pursuit, yelling:

"Here Wisty—down Maggy—down!"

Everybody together called greetings to the two dogs, and it sounded pretty loud.

"I named them," Aunt Olivette shouted at Ellen. "After my flowers. Wisty is short for wisteria, and Maggy for magnolia."

Ellen, trying to hear what Aunt Olivette was saying to her, forgot the dogs, and the next thing she knew she was looking straight into the yawning red cavern of Maggy's mouth about an inch from her face. Two rows of very white, very sharp, glistening teeth ran all the way back, and try as she might, she couldn't altogether dodge the long moist tongue. The dog's two heavy front paws pushed at her shoulders and it was all Ellen could do to keep her feet. Kurt and Clyde both jumped to help her. Aunt Olivette poked at the big dog's ribs gently with the silver-headed cane.

"Behave, Maggy," Clyde commanded, but Kurt got his hand under the dog's collar and yanked.

"That's a little too much affection, Maggy. Are you all right, Miss Marshall?"

Breathless and laughing, Ellen said she was.

"In the distance, I thought they were a couple of the ponies."

Aunt Olivette and Paul Jean were in the lead now, and Ellen walked on between the two men. Another five minutes and she stopped short with a cry of delight.

"They're gold—pure gold," she exclaimed.

"There you see fifteen golden palominos," Paul Jean told her proudly. He whistled, and two of them, arching their necks, started a canter across the pasture, long cream-colored manes and tails flying.

"They know they're supposed to show off before visitors and they love it," Kurt said.

When the saddles were brought, Aunt Olivette had changed her mind about riding out with them. She said she'd go back to the house; she'd had enough excitement for one day.

Almost from the first, Clyde and Paul Jean rode along together, deep in discussion about improvements and repairs that Clyde wanted to make on the stables and other buildings.

Ellen and Kurt cantered along side by side after them and stopped at one of the buildings while the others went inside.

"Would you like to ride along the beach, Miss Marshall?" Kurt asked. "That's where I like it best."

"Oh, I would," Ellen answered.

They left the buildings and followed a bridle path bordered by big pines that looked like parasols opened to shade them from the sun. The horses were full of life and frolic.

"They're playful," Kurt said. They came to a broad, green meadow.

"Dare you—or are you good enough for some jumps?" Kurt cried.

"Taken—and double-dare you."

Ellen wheeled her horse, set it at a stone wall, and bounded over it beautifully. Kurt followed. Then a shallow ditch—and a deeper one, until finally they were out on the hard-packed sand of the beach.

"Do you like the little mare?" Kurt galloped up to Ellen.

"She's a sweetheart," Ellen answered. "And she's so photogenic, she ought to be in pictures," she added, laughing up at him. She felt excited. Being with Kurt changed everything.

"You both should be in pictures," Kurt said seriously. "You've no idea what a picture you made as you took that stone wall back there. Where did you learn to ride like that?"

"Dad and Mother had a little ranch where we used to go summers," she said. "I had my own pony when I was five. Later I rode with the girls at school."

They trotted for a while, the horses even sloshing through the water in places, for it was low tide and calm. The waves tumbled about, far out beyond the promontory. Sometimes the beach got very narrow as they went along, and the rocks on one side were steep and high. They had to ride single file.

"Don't slide into the Atlantic Ocean back there," Kurt called to her.

"Not a chance," she shouted gaily.

Soon the beach widened out into a circular space, the sand white and warm from the sun, rimmed all around by the rocky formation. Kurt dismounted and came back.

"My hide-out," he said, and held up his arms for her.

Of the whole day—and it had all been pretty wonderful—Ellen remembered the next half-hour most vividly that night; and she knew she would remember it the rest of her life. Kurt found a flat rock for her to sit on, and then threw himself on the sand at her feet. They both watched the spanking-white sails of a small boat way off on the water.

"Your hide-out?" Ellen questioned, as Kurt had not spoken again.

"That's what I call this inlet. At low tide it's all white and clean, as you see it, but when the tide comes in, it's just part of that old ocean out there."

"Why do you need a hide-out?" Ellen asked him after a while.

"Oh, I come here for a few quiet laughs at myself sometimes." He spoke casually enough, but Ellen detected an edge of bitterness. "Life does queer things to us."

He means his wife, she thought, but said nothing.

"It wasn't always that way. Before I was married I used to ride out here just for the view, or because I liked the gallop along the beach, or felt like bucking the elements or—something."

He was drawing little patterns in the sand with his riding crop as he talked.

"Later on I asked Beatrice to ride out with me once or twice, but she hates the sea; says she's afraid of it. She doesn't care for horseback riding, either."

Suddenly he looked full at her, as if just looking deep into her eyes was what he longed to do above everything else. A strand of her ebony hair whipped straight across her face and clung there, because her skin was damp from the spray. She started to put up her hand to brush it back, but kneeling quickly, he said:

"Let me."

Matter-of-factly, but very gently, he tucked the strand back of her ear.

"Like a length of black satin ribbon," he said.

"The wind is coming up," she said, almost inaudibly.

He dropped a hand on the rock on either side of her, while his eyes still held hers.

"Isn't this going to be great—having you here? You'll ride with me, won't you, sometimes? And we can swim. You like to swim?"

He was like a boy asking a schoolgirl for a date.

As they were riding back, he said, "You know, it's the strangest thing. I've never before had anyone with me at the hide-out."

YOURS, WITH LOVE

Later on he spoke again. "I'm glad Beatrice didn't come out when I asked her to."

"I'm sorry your wife is so ill," Ellen said.

Instantly something happened; as if at the moment she uttered the words "your wife," a long-suppressed bitterness took possession of him. He had spoken of Beatrice himself, or Ellen would never have mentioned her. But her voice saying "your wife" seemed to unnerve him.

"Snap it up," he ordered roughly, and set his horse at a gallop.

When they got back to the stables they found that Clyde and Paul Jean had returned to the house. In the station wagon going home, Kurt said:

"Swim with me some morning?"

"Oh, yes. I would like that."

"Seven too early?"

"Seven it is," Ellen told him.

"Some day soon, then."

Laughing, in anticipation, they sprinted toward the house to change for dinner. As they entered the arbor that led to the side enrance, a shadowy figure in black rose and waited for them. They both slowed to a walk at once. It was Beatrice.

"Hello, there," said Kurt as they approached her.

Silence met this effort. When Ellen thought she couldn't stand it another minute, the woman said:

"You'd think you had to hide things from me, Kurt. You might have told me you were all riding out to the stables."

"But you never ride—" he started to protest.

"It's a good thing I haven't any curiosity," she interrupted. She turned toward the house, Kurt and Ellen following, not quite knowing what to do.

After a few steps, Beatrice came back and stopped directly in Ellen's path. She grasped a handful of the black curls that the wind had tossed into a silky mass. Disdainfully, she flung them back.

"If I were a hired employee, I'd find a neater way of arranging my hair. I'll expect you to do so while you're employed here."

Kurt's face went white.

"You're forgetting Miss Marshall is employed by Paul Jean, aren't you?" He grasped Beatrice by the arm.

"It's quite all right, Mr. Hollister," Ellen said. "I don't mind."

She streaked past them both, to the house. But she was afraid, just a little, of the anger she heard unleashed in the shrill words flung after her as she fled.

"Oh, so you don't mind—don't you? I'll see to it that you do mind."

"Stop it—stop it, I say," she heard Kurt's blaze of fury. "I'm sick to death of you!"

YOURS, WITH LOVE

"What in hell have you done to yourself?" was Paul Jean's lusty greeting as Ellen came quietly into the breakfast room the next morning. She had twisted her black curls into a tight bun on top of her head and pinned it securely. Her decision had been made last night, after a storm of tears.

Kurt Hollister is undergoing a terrible ordeal, she had told herself. I must help him in every way I can. A spinster hair-do is a minor sacrifice.

Kurt had been talking earnestly to Paul Jean, but when she appeared, both men jumped up and came over to her.

"You *couldn't* have taken Beatrice seriously, Miss Marshall," Kurt said. "She didn't mean—"

Paul Jean simply reached over and took out one hair pin after another. The curls tumbled to her shoulders.

"You looked as if one of grandfather's Indians had scalped you," he thundered. "What brought on all this?" He turned first to Kurt, then back to Ellen.

"Beatrice advocates hair styling along severe lines for Miss Marshall," Kurt explained.

"The hell she does," roared Paul Jean. "Come and have your coffee, Ellen. Get that nonsense out of your head. I'm your boss," he fumed.

"That Beatrice, Kurt! My patience is giving out, I'm warning you." He pounded the table. The next minute, however, he leaned back in his chair, the big laugh booming out.

"Here we are, two grown men and an intelligent girl, while our stockholders wait, Kurt near to missing his plane for Chicago, sitting around discussing my secretary's hair-do." He shouted with glee. When he could speak, he said sharply:

"Let Beatrice sweat it out, both of you. Jealous of your looks, Ellen; but I like 'em. Now let's drop it."

He and Kurt took up their discussion again. Kurt was catching a plane for Chicago, Ellen heard, leaving that day, to be gone perhaps a week. Then came more instructions to Kurt; he snapped a brief case shut, and was gone.

"See you," he said to them both from the door.

In the library, ready for dictation, Ellen glanced out of the windows. It had begun to rain, hard. Paul Jean was still going through his mass of papers, finding a place to start. There was a fire in the fireplace and he suddenly got up to give it a few vigorous jabs. The sparks flew and the logs blazed.

"Gets all-fired chilly so near the water. That's better. Now for a good day's work, Ellen."

When he said work, that's exactly what he meant. He dictated straight through until noon, with only occasional stops while he searched for some special

YOURS, WITH LOVE

reference among his notes. Ellen's hand was getting stiff from the continuous writing.

Paul Jean's dictation was easy to take down. He spoke reasonably fast, and when he wanted to emphasize something, he would pound down on his desk with his fist at each word. He was describing the "dry-washing" of gold, and he got especially forceful:

" . . . the men used wooden bowls, hewn out of solid blocks, (pound.) Into these they put the sand which contained the gold, (thump.) They held these bowls in their hands, (pound)—and threw the contents into the air, (pound.)"

He stopped for breath. Ellen looked up. Jeffers was standing at the door. Ellen saw him, but Paul Jean had his back to him. The butler rapped discreetly. In his hand he had a small silver tray with a letter on it. Paul Jean swung around and pounced on him.

"What's this? What have you got there, Jeffers?"

"It's for Miss Marshall, sir." The man, showing surprising dexterity, got past Paul Jean's outstretched hand.

"It's come by special delivery, sir, or I would never have interrupted."

Ellen took the letter and laid it quietly on the back of her desk. It was from Mabilla; she had seen the Westchester postmark.

"Aren't you going to read it?" Paul Jean asked.

"It's from my stepmother, Mr. Hollister. It can wait. I'm sure it isn't important."

"Where's your curiosity, young lady? Open the damned thing and see what's in it."

Ellen laughed and tore open the envelope.

"Please excuse me," she said. Then, eyes glued to the words as under a spell, Ellen read Mabilla's letter:

Dear Ellen,

It's not too bad here—even if I am passing out milk and bread-and-butter sandwiches to twenty of Aunt Margaret's kids every afternoon. They're from an orphans' home; two busloads, with a girl counselor and a man counselor—every day. AM lets them romp, she calls it, all over the place. She wants to join in the youth movement and that's about as far as she can go at her age, ha—ha!

The man counselor is cute. He wears white flannel pants and a turtle neck blue sweater, and such muscles—he plays baseball with the little boys.

But one of the bus drivers—that's for me. What I mean is, now don't misunderstand, he's so sympathetic about my recent loss, your late father, I refer to.

This is the life, kid. I wouldn't like it, though, between you and me and the lamppost, without the buses driving up, like the breath of life, every day. Winters must be fierce; nothing, but just nothing going on.

On and on she went, until the signature,
Your ever loving stepmother,
Hoping you are the same,
Mabilla.

Unnerved completely, Ellen sprang up and went over to the rain-swept windows. The letter had fallen to the floor.

"Heavens, my dear, you're upset. Let's see, what's all this? You must let me help."

Paul Jean picked up the letter. Ellen flashed back, involuntarily, to get it. He mustn't read it. Then she changed her mind. What did it matter? He might as well know.

"Please read it, Mr. Hollister. How could my father ever marry such a woman?" Her voice broke.

She went back to the window and Paul Jean read the letter through. Then he, too, came and looked out at the rain.

"Your own mother died when you were small, Ellen?"

"When I was twelve. After that Father and I were always together, except for the time I was away at school. I never thought he would marry again."

"Look here, Ellen. Let's try to think this thing out. I know a lot about life, maybe too much. Perhaps it's like this. Maybe before we're born we're all damned to live out our lives under certain general headings. You're in one category. I'm in another. The woman your father married—I can see this woman, Ellen. She's warm, expansive in her affection, takes everybody to her big heart, more or less. Some more, of course." He chuckled, and Ellen's head went up.

"There," said Paul Jean, "I've made you mad. That's a good counterirritant for tears. Seriously, though, Ellen, don't you see that your stepmother really does like human beings? She speaks of caring for the children. She dishes out their bread and milk, just the way she dishes out smiles to the bus driver. Liking everybody is a good trait, and makes up for a lot of other things." He paused a moment. Then, "She's out of your life now, Ellen. Forget her. Come on, let's eat."

Paul Jean and Ellen lunched alone. They worked on the book most of the afternoon. Finally, Paul Jean told her:

"I wish you'd return some of these files that we've finished with to the vault in the New York office, and bring back some others. I'll give you the keys and you go get them out of the secret archives, as I call 'em. Miss Winters will take care of you. She can help you better than I could myself."

He left the room, announcing that he was going out to his beloved horses. He always went to see them personally if there was a storm. Ellen remained in the library, putting things away, and by the time she had finished the room was heavy with gloom, for the rain had not yet let up.

The lights had not yet been turned on when she went out into the hall. It was lonely. Ellen glanced into the deserted drawing room. She still knew very little about the house.

The thick carpets muffled her footsteps; she made no sound at all as she moved about. The ceilings were so high; the shadows were so deep. She thought of Beatrice, apprehensively. She hoped she would never meet her when she was alone like this.

With a feeling of relief she turned back to the hall, where a fire was crackling in the fireplace. Ellen felt a little cheered by the friendly fire. She didn't feel quite so lost—and ahead of her was the familiar main staircase. In a few seconds she was halfway up.

A rush of heavy footfalls in the hall below her broke abruptly into Ellen's still half-frightened thoughts. Her hand reached out for the carved balustrade as she turned to see a young man behind her on the stairs, taking them three at a time. Was he after her? She gripped the banister with both chilled hands, looked him straight in the eye, and waited for whatever was going to happen.

The young man leaped right on by, never wasting a look on her.

"Flossie in?" floated back from the direction of

the long legs and flying arms above her.

"I don't know. Her rooms are right—" Ellen was tossing the words upward at his retreating back, for the young man had not paused at all. His passage had been so swift that Ellen had only a hazy impression of length and leanness, and a face wearing an expression that could only be described as grim. Without bothering to slow down, the stranger cut her short.

"I know where Flossie's rooms are," he said loudly.

Ellen, feeling as if she had been slapped, followed him along the wide corridor. He did indeed know where Flossie's rooms were, for he went straight to her door.

To her astonishment, he opened Flossie's door without knocking, without even an instant's hesitation. Apparently Flossie was in the sitting room, which opened from the hall.

"Get out!" she shouted, by way of greeting. "Get out of here! I told you I never wanted to see you again!"

Ellen could hear the young man's reply before the door closed.

"Shut up!" was what he said.

Ellen moved on to her own room. So that was Flossie's husband. The situation seemed a dangerous one. She wondered uneasily if she ought to warn someone that Flossie's husband, gone berserk, was in the house. But she had been warned that first night that Flossie and her husband were always fighting. She shrugged and decided to let events take their course.

Just before dinnertime, Ellen, standing in a corner of the great hall and examining through glass doors a collection of old ivory, heard Paul Jean's booming voice. He had come out of the library, evidently, in time to meet Flossie and her husband as they descended the stairs together.

"Aren't you staying to dinner, you two?"

"Flossie's anxious to get home," said the young man, with an air of finality.

Ellen glanced at Flossie, expecting at least a minor outburst at this high-handed behavior. But Flossie was clinging to her husband's arm, and now for a minute she laid her cheek against his sleeve. She came hardly to his shoulder, Ellen observed, and with her fair head nestled against the youth's dark sleeve, she looked so remarkably like a white kitten that Ellen would not have been surprised to hear her purr.

And this was Flossie, the untamed, and, Ellen had decided, untamable!

"Come on." Her husband yanked his arm away and extended his hand to Paul Jean. "Good-bye, sir."

"Good-bye, Charles, my boy," boomed Paul Jean.

Flossie threw her arms around Paul Jean's neck and kissed him softly. Paul Jean held her close for a minute. "Take good care of her, Charles," he said, over her head.

But Charles was already halfway to the door. Flossie slipped out of Paul Jean's arms, ran after Charles, and caught his hand, as he strode to the door, flung it open and went out, with Flossie in tow. Neither looked back.

"Masterful young pup, that Charles," Paul Jean chuckled. "Good for what ails that beautiful brat of ours."

❖❖ 5 ❖❖

"Miss Marshall? I'm Martha Winters."

The tall, gray-haired woman spoke in a crisp voice. Ellen had presented herself at Kurt Hollister's office, following Paul Jean's directions.

Miss Winters read the note Ellen handed to her.

"Sit down, Miss Marshall. Mr. Hollister says that he would like me to go over some of the data with you while you're here. Will you wait just a little while until I get my mail out of the way?"

"Certainly," Ellen said. "I'll sit over by the window where I won't disturb you."

She stole a glance at the woman several times as she rapidly slit open envelopes, made notes. She was smart-looking in every detail. Whether she was thirty-five or forty-five, Ellen could not tell.

The iron-gray hair was shining, beautifully groomed. The tall, spare figure was neat, almost painfully so, in a dark-blue tailored suit, with white collars and cuffs. She snapped her glasses, fastened to her lapel with a black ribbon, on and off her aquiline nose nervousely, between letters.

Finally, Miss Winters pushed a buzzer and a stenographer came in. She introduced her to Ellen.

"Oh, it's you today, Milly. Miss Marshall, this is Milly James."

The stenographer was a neat little thing, all skin and bones, but she looked competent. She quickly seated herself beside the cream-colored desk and got her notebook opened in one swoop before the blast of Miss Winters' runaway dictation.

The dictation went on. Ellen glanced at her watch. More time went on; so did the dictation. That was strange. This woman, a secretary herself for years, knew she was making Ellen waste all this time. She must be doing it on purpose. But why?

Ellen had arrived at ten. Now it was almost twelve. The little secretary, brown head bent, was making her thin fingers fairly fly over the pages of her notebook. The telephone rang. Miss Winters answered it and, getting up, said:

"I'll take it in Mr. Hollister's office."

Ellen, poring over a magazine, the minute the door closed heard a guarded, "P-s-st-tt!"

She looked up. The little stenographer whispered.

"You the Miss Marshall who lives out at the Hollister place?"

"Yes, I'm helping Mr. Paul Jean Hollister write his book."

"Oh, brother, has old Sourpuss got it in for you! She kept them records a lifetime; now you get the job."

Before Ellen could say a word the girl held up a hand, finger to her lips. "Sh-s-s-hh—here she comes."

Miss Winters came in, glancing at her wrist watch.

"I'm so sorry," she said to Ellen, "but I have to take this client of ours to lunch. He's from out of town. Perhaps you could have lunch with Milly. When you get back—I'll be late, of course—perhaps she could show you something about the files. Get to work as soon as you get back; the lunchtime is one hour." Miss Winters departed. In sheer astonishment, Ellen sat still, the magazine open in her lap.

Milly spoke up. "You stay here till I get my chapeau—that's French for hat," she giggled. "She wants us to hold our breath till she gets back, Miss Marshall. I've been here six years but I'm getting married next month, so she can't scare me any more. We'll go to lunch and I'll give you the lowdown on that one."

When they were seated at a restaurant table,

Milly started to talk, and she couldn't be stopped.

"Old Sourpuss is nuts about Mr. Hollister. Not the young one, Kurt, but Mr. Paul Jean. She started to work for him when she was twenty. He's a bachelor yet. And she in there tryin' all that time! Why, she even made some trips with him out to the mines long ago, when he still worked at engineering, out to California. That's where they got all them files that Sourpuss has been keeping all these years. They're Mr. Hollister's grandfather's notes and letters, and his father's, now his own. They rate them awful high. Historical value, they call it.

"Mr. Hollister's health got bad, and he couldn't come in to the office for a long time. But you should have seen her when he first got afflicted. I never did hear what's he's got—"

Having caught a deep breath, Milly went on:

"He was home for a year—resting, they said. Then when he gets ready to write the book at last, he ups and gets a new secretary. And when she saw you today—you're pretty gorgeous, Miss Marshall, I don't have to mention that."

"You're very kind," Ellen said, embarrassed.

"Think nothing of it," Milly replied airily.

"I think our hour is up, Milly. Shall we go?"

"Jeepers, will you look at the time, and you don't know the half of it, Miss Marshall."

Milly worked fast and accurately, so much so

that Ellen had almost all she needed by the time Miss Winter returned at a quarter to four. The room where the records were kept was the room Ellen had noticed when she met Kurt for that first interview, the one with the walls lined with books from floor to ceiling. The old records Paul Jean wanted were kept in a chest of locked drawers built into the wall. Milly told her the books were all about mining as well. Miss Winters did not come in to speak to her, but stayed in her own office. Finally, Ellen said to Milly:

"That's all I can carry in this brief case. If Mr. Hollister wants me to bring some more, I'll come back tomorrow. You have been so helpful, Milly. Thank you so much."

"Pleased, I'm sure," little Milly beamed.

Ellen went out to Miss Winters' office, but the secretary had a paper of some sort before her and did not look up. Ellen stopped briefly at the door.

"Good-bye, Miss Winters," she said. "Thank you."

"You're quite welcome."

Ellen caught her train, and was glad to sit still for a while and think, although she didn't know what to think about some things. There was Miss Winters, for instance.

After dinner that night Paul Jean said he would take the papers Ellen had brought and see if they were ready for more dictation the next day. They went through them together and he said he needed more data; that she'd better go into New York again the next day.

In her room a little later, Ellen, faced with another meeting with Miss Winters, thought that some of the fine salt air from down by the sea wall would do her good.

The moon made daylight of the whole grounds. Walking over the soft clipped grass of the terraces she was glad she had not tried to go to sleep yet, and miss all this. She wondered a little about Kurt. When would he be back? She walked slowly through the garden where she took dictation, past the sunken pool, and on along a gravel path.

Somehow I never feel that I'm alone when I think of Kurt, she mused.

There were sounds about, too, that were quite new to her, but she did not feel in the least afraid. As she walked under the pines, night birds hovered overhead and frogs kept up a muffled "jug-a-rum," deep in their husky throats. A few fleecy clouds floated across the sky and a full moon wandered in and out through them. Ellen put up both hands to push back her hair, to let the warm breeze blow full on her face.

"Throwing some radar at that old moon?" a man's voice asked softly. Two arms went round her waist and drew her back to a broad shoulder and held her tight. Unable to move at first, Ellen managed the next moment to turn her head to look up at the man—Clyde.

"Mr. Hollister!"

Ellen struggled to unlock the strong fingers clasped around her slim waist. Then just as suddenly as he had embraced her, Clyde let her go, so that she almost lost her balance.

"This is unpardonable, Mr. Hollister."

"I know—I know. But must you always cross my path so charmingly? Like the night you came into my arms to dance, the first night you were here? We had to meet, Angel. It was meant."

Sharp words suggested themselves vaguely to Ellen, but she did not say any of them. She did not speak at all. Clyde was silent, too, arms braced against the sea wall. The quick anger that had flared in her toward him died, as he turned deep gray eyes, that looked black now, upon her.

"What do you believe a man is born for?" he asked.

"It means different things to different men—living, I mean," she said, after a moment's hesitation. She must not be juvenile about this.

"That is exactly what people blame me for," he said, his voice tense. "For being myself."

He stooped so he could look into her eyes, then placed both hands at her waist and lifted her to the sea wall.

"I want you where I can see you. I want you to look at me and tell me you will form your own opinion of me, judge me as you find me. Just as if we were the only two people left in the world, as now. There isn't another soul for miles."

Ellen looked up at the endless sky. She heard the thud of the waves against the beach. She could not explain how she regarded this demanding, dominating man.

"You are exciting, baffling, gloriously beautiful," Clyde said. "Give me your promise to make up your own mind about me—promise?"

Surely this man would stir any girl's imagination. Violent, undisciplined, his lean handsome face was close, his eyes darkly on hers.

Ellen forced a casual tone. "I promise, but I think I should know something about you. Will you tell me?"

He gripped her hand, but she felt his fingers tremble. He vaulted lightly to the wall beside her. She started to withdraw her hand.

"No," he said. "Hold my hand. And look at me," he ordered. "I can tell what you are thinking if I can see your eyes."

After a moment he said, quite simply, "I love you, you know."

"Please—please." Ellen made an attempt to leave.

"No, stay here. I wanted you to know, from the first. I have loved woman's beauty before, but now I love a woman as well as her beauty. I knew the moment I saw you."

Ellen said nothing. Clyde was silent for a moment.

Then—"I was kicked out of one college after another, shipped on a tramp steamer, owned a string of polo ponies. I've been an actor, a bond salesman—two days, that was. I've been in prison, not in this country, in South America. I fly, have my own plane here. I want to take you up some day soon. I've lived in Paris, studied art. I'm a damned good architect, even Paul Jean will tell you that. And I've been lonely, all my life long, in spite of crowds of people."

He took her hands and placed them on either side of his face and held them there.

"Now I have you."

"If you make love to me, Mr. Hollister," Ellen said, "I shall have to leave this house."

He jumped down and lifted her from the wall and held her. He pressed his lips to hers—long and hard.

"Come," he said then, catching her hand in his. "I will not make love to you again like this."

On the wooden steps going over the rocks, he caught her roughly by the shoulders.

"I am not the man to take little snatches of stolen love from you—I want all your love."

Then he walked her, almost too fast for her to

keep up with him. Halfway across the terrace he stopped, kissed her hands, first one and then the other, very gently.

"Good night, Angel." He was gone.

Ellen walked the few remaining steps over the grass slowly. Did a slender black figure glide on before her toward the side entrance?

The great front door was open and Ellen sped up the grand staircase, uncertain, exhausted all at once. If that shadow had been Beatrice, she would, without a doubt, tell Paul Jean or Kurt what she had seen, even some things she hadn't seen.

For the first time since she had been at Hollister House, Ellen closed the windows that looked out over the sea, now bathed in brilliant moonlight. And she pulled the rose-colored draperies over them. She buried her face in her pillow.

Had she been wrong to listen to Clyde? If only her father were near. If she could see Kurt; but of course she would not tell him about Clyde. But if she could just see him—be near him.

I've got to be ready when the chauffeur comes to take me to that eight-seven train in the morning. After all, I'm working here. I'm not being paid to take strolls in the moonlight with ardent young men, she admonished herself.

At last she fell into a troubled sleep

❖❖ 6 ❖❖

When Ellen got to Miss Winters' office the following morning she was met by Milly James, a particularly impish grin on her little face.

"Miss Winters will not be in today," she announced. "She has a bad headache. Isn't that too, too bad?" she asked gleefully.

"Yes, indeed," Ellen answered, but she had to turn her back to hide her smile at the girl's high spirits.

"Now we can really get some work done on those files, Miss Marshall."

Milly James was really a treasure. She showed Ellen about the files and the method used in filing the different kinds of records. She showed her how the books were arranged on the shelves according to a method that made locating the information Paul Jean wanted easy.

About the middle of the morning Aunt Olivette telephone Ellen and told her that she was going to take her to the Singers Club for luncheon.

"We'll go there and eat all the gooey things that aren't good for us, Marshall," she jubilated over the phone. "Wait there at the office for me."

The next thing Ellen heard was a ringing snatch of song:

"Lover, come back to me-e-e—" as Olivette evidently walked away, leaving the phone lying on the table instead of replacing it in its cradle.

"I heard her singing. That was Miss Olivette, Mr. Paul Jean's sister, wasn't it, Miss Marshall?" Milly asked.

"Yes," Ellen said. "I'm to have lunch with her."

"Oh, she's just the grandest lady. You've no idea, Miss Marshall, what she does for the girls here. Every Christmas every one of us gets a check, that's outside of the bonus we get from the company. And twice while I've been here she was in town and came here just to sing Christmas carols for us."

In the taxi, on the way to the club, Olivette said, "You know, Marshall; I'm taking you to the club just to show you off. I think I'll do a lot of it this winter when my friends get back to town. It will make Beatrice furious, my dear." The silver-headed

YOURS, WITH LOVE 89

cane tapped the window just behind the chauffeur's ear. "Take it easy, man; we're going to lunch, not to a fire."

At the club people came up in twos and threes and singly to speak to Olivette. She had many friends, Ellen thought, the way people crowded to speak to her. Her sharp wit kept all within earshot in gales of laughter.

Before dessert Ellen had to beg to be excused. There was such a lot yet to be done in the office.

"That's too bad, Marshall. I thought you could come along to my dressmaker's with me. Some other day we'll get in a day's shopping—I love gadding about."

Olivette stayed on with her friends and Ellen hurried back to the office. Milly was busy typing out a cross index for Ellen's own use.

"You keep this with you and you'll never have to ask Old Sourpuss for anything again. You won't even have to ask for me—unless you'd like to have me," she finished wistfully.

"Of course, I'll always ask for you, Milly."

At that moment the door in the big office back of them opened and quick steps crossed the room. Milly held her hands suspended in mid-air above the typewriter keys, to listen. Ellen, being nearest, went to the open door, and stood there in surprise, facing Kurt Hollister.

He spoke first.

"Miss Marshall, how nice. Getting data for Uncle Paul Jean? Is Miss Winters helping you?"

Milly, recovered, came from behind Ellen.

"Miss Winters is not here. She has a headache."

"I'm sorry to hear that," Kurt said. "Miss Marshall, I'll have to ask for help again, I'm afraid. I'm in town to have some important forms drawn up. Will you—?"

"Certainly, Mr. Hollister," said Ellen, trying to keep the warmth out of her eyes and voice. "I've almost finished with Mr. Paul Jean's work."

"I'm afraid you're letting yourself in for some hard work, Miss Marshall," Kurt said, as Ellen seated herself beside him at the big desk. "It may take an hour or so this evening, too."

Ellen looked up and smiled.

"I'll be glad to stay as long as you need me," she told him.

Ellen was wearing a simply cut gown of soft summer material, the same violet blue of her eyes. It clung to her figure, showing the tall, slender lines and youthful curves. There was no ornament on the dress; she wore no jewelry except her wrist watch. Her beautiful tapering legs, nylon-clad, were crossed at the knees. Without even suspecting that he was doing nothing but looking at the picture she made, Kurt did just that. He sat and looked at Ellen. Milly James had gone out and closed the door and they were alone together. The atmosphere was one of dignity and quiet, and, as he was now thinking, beauty. He did not formulate any phrases; his feeling was deeper than words. What was it that compelled him, at this moment above all others, to think of Beatrice, and the absence of the slightest spark of emotion for her—for so long?

To break away from the thought, he spoke, more abruptly than he had meant to do.

"This contract is a particularly involved one, Miss Marshall. I have to think it out."

"Shall I go?" Ellen asked, rising at once. Standing there, close to him, Kurt knew without reservation that she was the most beautiful girl he had ever seen. He said hurriedly—most of all he did not want her to leave—"No—no. Stay right there."

He got up and walked over to the wide windows. They were high above the noise, and the rumble of sound that came up seemed far away. Kurt looked down upon the slow, winding lines of automobile tops, cautiously moving up one side of the street and down the other. He looked out at the fabulous geometric piles that were New York's skyscrapers; at the clustered dots that were people, moving endlessly. The orderliness of this multitude of people was amazing, he thought for the hundredth time. Paul Jean had once said, looking down from that same window:

"People conform; they follow the rules. Good

Lord, put that many people together without a set code of conduct and they'd kill each other."

Kurt laughed aloud. That was just what he needed, the thought of Paul Jean. He defied any man to think of Paul Jean as he knew him and not get his feet on the ground. He went back to his desk, ready for work.

"All set, Miss Marshall?" he called so brightly that Ellen went along with his mood.

"Ready," she told him, pencil poised at mock attention. "Is this to be an endurance test, or are we trying for speed?"

They both laughed outright.

A thought came to Kurt.

"Why didn't I think of this before?" he burst out. "I want to *talk* to you about the new problems our superintendent presented to me in Chicago. I want you to talk to me about them; I don't want to dictate until we've both talked it out."

He got up, offered her a cigarette, lit it, and took one himself.

"Get up, Miss Marshall. Come over to the window here with me. Walk about, suit yourself, so we can talk."

Ellen went to the window and stood looking out with him. Kurt's voice was gentle as he started:

"It's too much, the responsibility for human lives, for one man alone to decide. With you standing here beside me, giving your opinion, clear-eyed and with a fresh outlook, it will help immeasurably. How I wish you could have been out to the mines. I make two trips a year, since Paul Jean stopped going."

"I would like to see the mines—above everything," Ellen told him. "Doing the book with Mr. Hollister has already put me in touch with the early problems of the miners."

"Of course it has, of course. Those early years were plenty brutal. And that's just what we try constantly to rectify; we are still trying, several generations later, to get the workers in the gold fields to realize that they are not a helpless, hapless, forgotten herd, under bosses who want to bury all the gold they mine in their private back yards."

"And it isn't easy for you to prove that you want happiness for them—that you want to give them courage?" Ellen prompted.

"That's it exactly. Just hearing you say it makes it simpler. The superintendent I met in Chicago has suggestions along welfare lines for the miners, more safety installations to be approved, and—"

Kurt stood looking down at her in the bright sun streaming through the window.

"And he wants you to raise the take-home pay in their envelopes?" Ellen suggested.

She thought, "His eyes do shine when they look at me."

"I might have known you would understand," he said. "I must have been sure when I started to tell you these things."

"And what else?" Ellen asked. "More problems?"

"Paul Jean," Kurt said at once. "He's a stout fellow of the old school. You know that yourself. He still thinks it's fun in a way to wrest a living from the hard cold ground with your bare hands. It isn't that he will mind the money when I dump this new spending plan in his lap; it's just that he thinks men ought to like to get in there and fight and sweat and suffer."

"How do you feel about it?" Ellen asked.

"I want to okay every last suggestion the superintendent made. He's on the ground, knows the men, and knows what they need. He's been with us for years, is honesty itself, and he knows his business.

"I'm trying to get you on my side," he continued after a moment. "I want you to agree with me; above all I want to hear what you think."

Before she knew it, Ellen was pouring out her ideas to Kurt. All she knew on the subject of gold mines was what she had gone through with Paul Jean in writing the book. All at once she checked herself, struck speechless by her own rashness.

But Kurt seized her hands. "Ellen—Ellen— Now I know what I'm going to write." He flung himself down at his desk.

"Come over here. By the way, it's Ellen and Kurt from now on?" He looked up on the question. Ellen nodded. "Say it like this," Kurt went on, then stopped, sorting papers on his desk.

"I can take it directly on the typewriter if you wish, Mr.—that is, Kurt."

As she said his name aloud for the first time, Ellen's eyes, darkly violet now, met his, and her face was radiant, but she was completely unaware of it. Kurt drew a deep, audible breath. Ellen sat down before the typewriter, set the carriage of the machine, ready to begin. Kurt hesitated; then, in a voice louder than necessary, plunged into his subject, the words coming easily after the first seconds, expressing exactly the terms he wished to set forth.

It did not take long. Kurt stood, his hand sometimes on the back of Ellen's chair as she took down what he dictated. She steeled herself to an outward calm, but she was almost unbearably aware of Kurt's nearness; for a little space of time life had a faster tempo, new meaning, vitality.

"How did we two ever accomplish so much in so short a time?" Kurt said at last. "I thought we'd be here on into the evening.

"Go on, get your hat," he ordered abruptly. "We'll have dinner together. We've only begun to talk about—things."

Obediently, Ellen went and got the blue hat,

made by an expert milliner from a scrap of the same material as her dress. When she came back and stood looking up at him, Kurt regarded her as he had before sometimes, she'd noticed, without a word.

"Come on," he said, almost roughly.

He took her to a dining room at one of his clubs. The food was superb, but Ellen did not notice. She remembered later only the gleam of the silver-covered dishes, the deftness of the waiter. She didn't know at all what she ate.

She listened to Kurt's deep voice, telling her of plans he had for the betterment of the miners. He spoke of himself, of playing polo, years back. He couldn't find the time for it now.

As he talked of the things that interested him most, Ellen, with almost a sense of shock, saw that this man, young, handsome, gifted in his profession —he was a lawyer, he told her—seemed to be weighted down with a burden, one that he bore impatiently. Gradually, as he talked, she had the impression that this burden had grown lighter.

After coffee had been served, he asked suddenly, "Do you believe there can be a close, lasting attraction between two people—a man and a woman, I mean—unless there is a definite mental sympathy?"

Then, seeing a smile lurking in Ellen's eyes, he hastened to clarify. "Let's say the man has brains and brawn, the girl charm and beauty. I do believe that lasting attachment, love itself, must have this firmer foundation of mental attraction as well."

Kurt told her he wished they could see a show together, but he was attending a late business meeting. He did not expect to get out to Hollister House for another day or two. He drove with Ellen to the station.

All the way home she thought of him. What an amazing man he was.

What would it be like if he kissed her?

Paul Jean had left word for Ellen to come to the library when she got in from New York, so she went there directly. He went through the data she had brought from the files and was delighted with it, and said so.

"Couldn't have done better myself, Ellen."

Ellen told him about having lunch with Olivette and an early dinner with Kurt.

"Yes," he said. "Kurt phoned me a little while ago and said you helped him out tremendously. What did we ever do before you came here, I wonder?"

"You're joking, Mr. Hollister," she said. She couldn't believe he meant it.

"Indeed I'm not joking, young lady. I'm in dead earnest. And while we're talking about you, I want you to take the best of care of yourself here.

If you need anything, ask for it. If you have problems, come to me or Olivette with them."

Ellen glowed and smiled at him. This had been a peculiar afternoon and evening—in such a joyous way.

Paul Jean went on.

"Tomorrow, dictation, all day if we feel up to it. The next day, get some of the typing done. I don't want to plow under the best secretary I ever had with too many notes."

"You'll spoil me, Mr. Hollister," Ellen said.

"Can't spoil your kind, Ellen. And Sunday, how would you like to go out for a sail in my boat?"

"The Sea Puss?" she sparkled up at him.

"The same. And when anyone mentions her name I demand tribute as my right, because I made that boat what she is today."

Paul Jean got up and put a hand on her shoulder to lead her to the door.

"Don't get me started on the love of my life, that old Sea Puss. That would mean an all night session. Good night, Ellen."

Ellen looked long at the rugged face, which in this light took on the appearance of a fine piece of sculpture. What dignity the man had. She felt it was a privilege to know him. Of course she could not say how she felt. Giving him a last fleeting glance of gratitude, she said, her voice low:

"Good night."

YOURS, WITH LOVE

Walking across the dimly shining floor of the main hall toward the grand staircase, Ellen was conscious of but one thing now. So much had happened, she was not able to think at all; all she knew was that she was blissfully tired.

"You have exquisite ankles, Angel."

Without getting up, Clyde's long, lean figure, in one of the high-backed chairs against the far wall, lounged forward so that both elbows rested on his knees. Ellen stood still.

"I've been sitting here for ages, waiting for Paul Jean to get through talking about that gee-whiz book of his." He didn't speak again for a moment. Then:

"Come over here. I have a gift for you." As she came slowly toward him he held out a bunch of fresh sweet peas. Not ordinary ones; they were orchid in color. Ellen had seen them in Olivette's garden.

"Did you ever in your life smell such a vigorous perfume?" he asked, holding out the fragrant flowers.

Ellen pressed them to her face.

"I knew it—I knew it," he exulted.

"What?" she questioned.

"They're the same color as your eyes at night, purple, a sort of pale purple."

Ellen, at a loss, said simply, "Thank you."

"You're going in to New York again tomorrow,

aren't you?" Then without waiting for her answer he went right on, "I'll meet you when you're through at the office. We'll have dinner. I'll get you an orchid, and we'll dance. And I'll have you in my arms," he finished, his voice husky.

"But I'm working here with Mr. Hollister all day tomorrow."

His mood changed so swiftly that Ellen's mind felt dizzy. His eyes were dark and intense.

"Why didn't you let me know you were going to New York both these other days?" he demanded. "You're cruel."

He flung the words at her, then left without even a backward glance.

I don't understand him at all. He's so dramatic. Ellen went slowly up the stairs to her room.

Again it was not easy to fall asleep.

❖❖ 7 ❖❖

It was very warm the next morning. While getting out her coolest blue and white print, Ellen noticed that the hem on her white gabardine skirt had come loose. Having nothing to mend it with, she took the skirt over her arm, intending to ask Jeffers, the butler, what one did about repairs here.

When she got downstairs she rang for him and showed him what she wanted done.

"Certainly, Miss Marshall," Jeffers said. "Come with me. We have a seamstress here in the house, Mary Gilly. She's the granddaughter of old Dominick, the head gardener."

Ellen followed the butler as he went to several places that appeared to be good guesses as to where a seamstress might be—the linen room, an immense place with row upon row of neatly folded household linen; a curtainless sitting room on the second floor where piles of material were strewn about, evidently waiting to be hemmed; finally, a sunny sewing room, fully equipped with two sewing machines, dress forms and the like, but no Mary Gilly. They went downstairs again, out to the garden, and located Dominick to ask him if he knew where his granddaughter was.

The old man, holding a cold pipe in his hand, came forward to meet them. When asked if he knew Mary's whereabouts, he pointed a trembling gnarled finger toward a pretty white cottage just within sight among the trees. But what surprised Ellen was that before he turned away she caught in the bleared, old eyes such a look of malevolence that she caught her breath.

"Sure. I know where she is. With him, over at the house. Fixing it up with paint and such like. Mr. Clyde—"

The hate in the shaking old voice seemed actually to burst right through the faded blue demin jacket he wore. He walked away without another word.

Why the fact that Clyde Hollister was helping Mary Gilly do over her house should cause such bitter agitation on her grandfather's part was something beyond Ellen's grasp. She caught herself staring speculatively after the dignified lone old figure, tired shoulders drooped. It was plain enough

YOURS, WITH LOVE

that there was some evil he wanted to smack at, lustily, as he would have in his youth, but the logic of the years told him he was powerless. Seeing that Jeffers was standing, too, watching Dominick go slowly down the path, Ellen spoke hastily.

"I can see the cottage from here, Jeffers. You may go back—and thank you."

"Yes, Miss, thank you, Miss," the man said and left her. Ellen followed the moss-grown path under the shady trees. Nearing the cottage, she heard shouts of laughter coming out through the open windows—a man's voice and a girl's. The man's, without a doubt, was Clyde Hollister's, the same voice that had spoken to her, intimately, so short a time before. Clyde was doing most of the talking. On the girl's part there were only little puffs of laughter for response.

It sounds as if he has found a more tractable companion. Ellen walked more slowly, reluctant to go on. She did not wish to intrude. Then she decided against turning back. She was still carrying the skirt with the sagging hem over her arm; she might as well leave it.

The man and girl, flat on the floor, busy with paint brushes, were not aware of their visitor as Ellen stood in the open doorway. Their feet pointed Ellen's way, and they only turned their heads far enough around every so often to look at each other as they worked and laughed. As Ellen watched, not liking to interrupt, the girl adroitly flapped herself over on her back, never glancing toward the door. Ellen could see her face now.

An overblown rose, and, like a flower, careless of her loveliness, Ellen thought. About my own age, nineteen or twenty, she guessed. No wonder Clyde finds her attractive. A man could span her waist with his hands. And those long, lithe legs, hard-muscled like a swimmer's, smooth and firm.

As she stood there, Ellen had a guilty feeling, as if she'd been deliberately eavesdropping. She rapped lightly on the door jamb, wishing she were anywhere at all except where she was. Clyde peered over his shoulder and yelled at the girl in order to penetrate her mirth.

"Heaven is on our doorstep, my lass. Shut up—and get up."

The girl reacted slowly. She raised herself as far as the hips and sat there with her two arms propping her up from the floor. She remained silent, regarding her visitor framed in the doorway. Ellen looked back into the face that had a doll-like quality; the big brown eyes were widely spaced, and blankly pretty.

Clyde bounded to his feet and crossed the room with a stride or two. It was such a tiny room, and he was so big. Ellen had stepped just inside, and as she stood there she had the uncomfortable feeling of being crowded, although there were only the three of them. Clyde was wearing a pair of white shorts and a longish jacket with two huge patch pockets, belted at the waist and open at the brown column of his throat.

Heavens, he's good-looking, Ellen couldn't help thinking.

"Hello there," Clyde said to her, his greeting low and intimate.

"Hello," she answered.

Ellen had almost forgotten the skirt she was carrying folded over her arm. Clyde, in the authoritative way that seemed characteristic of the Hollister men, took it away from her and held it up before him.

"Some mending?" he inquired, turning it carefully about. He discovered the torn hem.

"Your department, Mary." He turned toward the girl, and seeing her still sitting on the floor, became greatly annoyed. His expression changed, darkly.

"You're acting like a fool—get up."

Ellen watched him, fascinated. Mary did, too, and now she seemed too frightened to move. Clyde's face was set in white fury, out of all proportion to the simple fact that Mary remained seated on the floor when he'd told her to get up.

Mary Gilly, her beseeching eyes never leaving Clyde's face, her lower lip trembling faintly, still sat on the floor. And instead of going over to help her, which seemed such a natural thing to do, Clyde, not moving from where he stood, rolled Ellen's skirt up into a ball and threw it at Mary. It landed in her lap, but it barely missed striking her in the face. Then he turned abruptly and walked out of the house. Ellen went to the girl at once.

"Take your time about this, Mary. It's not important. The hem has to be caught in a few places. Take great big stitches—it really doesn't matter."

Ellen felt deep sympathy for this pretty childlike creature who had been shabbily treated before a stranger; and she blamed herself for the incident. Mary was standing beside her now, running her practiced fingers along the hem that was the cause of the whole thing.

"I'm so sorry," Ellen said.

"Oh, you mean about him, Clyde? He's highstrung. And he's been extra touchy lately, ever since . . ."

The girl's soft voice trailed off, making no attempt to finish the sentence. Her limpid eyes, which Ellen could only compare to those of a fawn that she'd once seen in the zoo, were disconcerting.

"Clyde didn't mean anything. I never mind what he does—really I don't."

The murmured words and downcast eyes showed Ellen as plainly as if Mary had said it—*I'm in love with him.*

Why, she's in love with Clyde. Ellen couldn't be mistaken. That explained the grandfather's anger at the man, too. And it was a shame. How could a man with Clyde's background and advantages have involved a simple girl like Mary Gilly, plainly no match for him in any way? Vaguely Ellen tried to think of some advice to give her, but decided it was useless. Even if she could think of anything to say about a man of Clyde's type, she wouldn't feel free to say it. Anyway, Mary wouldn't listen to a girl no older than herself. It was best to ignore what she had seen. It occurred to her that Mary didn't even know who she was. As brightly as she could, she said:

"I'm Ellen Marshall. I'm Mr. Hollister's secretary—that is, Mr. Paul Jean."

"Yes, I know, Miss Marshall. I'll finish the sewing and bring the skirt up to the house this evening."

And again, surprisingly, the girl seemed in irrepressibly high spirits; as if nothing unpleasant had happened at all. She was smiling radiantly as she waved good-bye to Ellen from the doorstep.

Ellen, half annoyed with herself, thought as she walked away, I'm losing my perspective, I guess. Evidently she doesn't care how Clyde treats her, just as she says. I was the one who minded, which is being pretty silly.

But she was angry with Clyde in spite of herself. A little later she had to smile, because as she walked along the narrow moss-covered path, all at once she realized she was actually stamping down on the soft stuff.

I'm being so foolish—and this moss would deaden the heaviest footfall. The thick pad of moss did blunt footfalls, Ellen was made aware within the next few moments, for although she didn't suspect anyone was near, a firm hand closed over hers from behind and held tight.

Momentum made Ellen take the next two steps without even looking around, her hand clasped by that other. Then she stopped and looked up into the cool gray of Clyde's eyes. She tried to withdraw her hand.

"Just your hand in mine. Do you mind so very much?"

"I do mind. Very much."

He did not let go of her hand, and fell into step beside her.

"This is wonderful," he said, after they had gone along a little way. Then he stopped and took both Ellen's hands. "Midnight hair, sapphire eyes—"

"Mr. Hollister," Ellen exclaimed. "You are forgetting, I think, that I am employed here. I have a job, and romancing is no part of it."

"I know, I know about your job. No one could miss it with Paul Jean broadcasting it every minute. But make a magic carpet of that job, Ellen. Make it take you to new places, new adventures. The broader your vision is, the better your job will be."

"It occurs to me you may have been broadening Mary Gilly's vision!" Ellen retorted.

She hadn't meant to mention Mary Gilly. She was frightened when she heard herself saying the words. Clyde grasped her roughly by the shoulders and bent down to look into her eyes. His own seemed to have gone colder and grayer—opaque.

"What did she tell you about me? Did she say anything about me?" He shook her a little when she hesitated in answering.

"Let go of my shoulders, Mr. Hollister," Ellen said, so sternly that he complied.

"Mary Gilly said nothing at all about you," she told him then. "I apologize for speaking as I did. It was just the expression of her eyes as she watched you go down the path. She's in love—"

"With me? Nonsense."

"It would be unfair—she's untutored."

"All women have instinct to go by where men are concerned, Ellen, tutored or not. What they do with their lives is always their own affair." He was suddenly irritable. "I'm sick of the thought of Mary Gilly. I want to talk about you. You know that. You're putting me off."

They were at the edge of the rose garden now and Clyde went to one of the bushes and picked a red rose.

"Wait," he called, as Ellen started to move on without him. She stopped.

He came over to her, stood close, touched the petals of the rose to his lips.

"My signature," he said with mock gallantry as he handed it to her. "I want to kiss you—you know that. But I won't, because I promised I wouldn't the other night. Not until you want me to." He said it gently.

But Ellen started across the terrace without answering. Clyde walked beside her until they reached the private side steps that led up to Beatrice's apartment. Stopping before it, he faced Ellen.

"When will you go up in my plane with me? I've been working on it and it's ready to take off. Make it tomorrow!"

"No," Ellen said, without looking at him, and went on alone. Just as she moved away, she heard Beatrice's voice from the top of the stairs.

"Is that you, Clyde? You're late, dear."

Ellen was conscious of a sense of shock. That word of endearment! But of course Clyde and Beatrice knew each other very well, living so long in the same house. Still, Beatrice had said he was late. It sounded as if he called on her regularly.

Paul Jean was waiting for her when Ellen finally reached the library. She started to explain about searching for Mary Gilly. He cut her short.

"I was late getting started myself. We can work hard to make up lost time."

They did, too. Except for time out for lunch, they worked all day. It was nearly five when Paul Jean looked at his wrist watch and said, almost sharply, to Ellen:

"What do you think? Is this book any blankety-blank good? The truth, now. I'll know if you're lying."

"Every line of it is interesting. How can you ask, Mr. Hollister? This last part you've just dictated—it makes me want to hear more."

"Good." He got his papers in some semblance of order and handed them to her.

"Tell you what. We'll work a full day tomorrow and the next let's play hookey—take a day's sail on my boat. Kurt wires me he expects to be here then and wants to talk things over with me. About his trip, I mean."

Paul Jean looked up at her keenly. "Says he'd like to have you sit in on our conference. What's he mean, young lady?"

"Oh, just that we talked about bettering conditions for the miners. I think I said more than I should when I talked with him in New York."

"Not at all, not at all, Ellen. I want to hear your views. From the first day I laid eyes on you I knew you were none of that glass-brained variety of female we meet so much. I knew that beautiful head of yours was set pretty level on your shoulders."

"I hope I deserve such confidence," Ellen began, but he stopped her.

"Tut, tut, Ellen. We Hollister men make up our own minds about things. The three of us will take that trip on the Sea Puss and we'll talk, without interference. Day after tomorrow."

❖❖ 8 ❖❖

"Hello," Kurt said, leaning on the banister at the foot of the stairs.

"Hello," said Ellen. She was wearing a white bathing suit, with her fingertip length bright blue box coat over her shoulders. She had her slacks in the little bag she carried, together with her sunglasses and compact. Her skin was already tanned a deeper apricot tone from her sessions with Paul Jean in the garden; her eyes sparkled up at Kurt.

He held out his hand to her. There was a tenseness about him as he stood waiting for her, unsmiling.

Ellen was a little breathless as he took her hand; he was so close to her. She hadn't expected to see him alone; she thought that Paul Jean would be with him. He had on white slacks and shirt, with the sleeves of a brilliant red sweater knotted around his throat. She had not realized how brown he was till she saw him in this morning sun, nor how blond his hair was.

"Cuppa coffee?" he asked, as they moved across the hall side by side.

"Cuppa coffee," she agreed, feeling like an echo. Was she going to keep on all day just repeating what he said? But Paul Jean arrived just then and after that nobody else had to talk.

"Was there ever another day like this?" he yelled at them. Barely catching his breath, "Jeffers—Jeffers!"—he bawled. "Got the hampers ready?"

The man appeared like magic. "In the station wagon, sir, and ready to go."

"Let's go—Ellen, Kurt."

Into the station wagon they went, then on a launch over to the schooner. Jerry, the chauffeur, came with them, and a young man who helped the cook came with the hampers.

"There she is, Ellen—the love of my life. Isn't she a beauty? An old-time coasting schooner, she is, no yacht, mind you. Not a civilized gadget on her, bless her. Look at her sails, look at her lines—beautiful, that's what—beautiful."

Ellen was laughing outright at his enthusiasm as Kurt helped her aboard.

Paul Jean sailed the Sea Puss himself, although

YOURS, WITH LOVE

two men who lived on the boat had everything in readiness. The schooner was two-masted and her sails ballooned as she leaned to the wind.

As Paul Jean had said, Ellen thought there could never have been a more perfect day for an ocean trip: dazzling sun, brilliant blue sky, with only a few handfuls of clouds drifting about. Feathers of white foam outlined the beach they had left behind them, and out here there were only gentle swells. Ellen lifted her face to the fresh, salty breeze and drew in deep breaths.

"Isn't this something?" Kurt asked.

"It's everything," Ellen answered. "All there is." Raising her eyes she was surprised to see that he was looking down at her, as if it were impossible for him to do otherwise. Something compelled his gaze, until, almost impatiently, as if playing for safety, he spoke.

"Come along. We'll get you a cabin—here. Mine is right next. Leave your coat. You'll want to get the sun." He disappeared into his cubicle of a cabin. When Ellen emerged from hers, he was already on deck, in a pair of red trunks, sprawled on the roof of a cabin.

"Come over here by me," he ordered.

"Grab yourself a cushion. This wood is uncommonly hard."

Ellen brought one for him, too, and they both stretched out on their backs in the sun. Paul Jean, in a pair of white linen trousers rolled up above his knees, his huge torso bare and sun-tanned to a deep mahogany, gave his undivided attention to his beloved boat.

The silence between Ellen and Kurt seemed oddly companionable. It was as if there were no need of words between them. They were alone—alone in a world of their own; a world of sun and sea, of warmth and happiness, no matter how long or short its duration.

Without preliminary Kurt began to speak, very slowly.

"Does it show weakness in a man, one, say, who has grown up as I have, accepting without question moral, financial, and social security, if when he finds all his safety suddenly blown up in his face, he doesn't know what to do? Does it mean that he isn't as strong as he thought he was? Suppose he realizes well enough that something must be done, but he cannot bring himself to face it. Is there something wrong with that guy's character?"

"No," whispered Ellen. "No."

She lay perfectly still, eyes closed against the glare of the sun. Then Kurt reached out a hand blindly, found her for a moment, as if he wanted to be sure she was there, then let it go.

After a while he said, so low she could hardly hear him, "Ellen."

"Yes, Kurt."

"It's as if someone had blasted a hole in the wall his kind of life had built around him, and all of a sudden, there he is, looking through it to another world. His own life becomes hateful to him then. Ellen—he's being dragged down, down. Can you tell him what to do?"

His head went down on his arms, folded now on his drawn-up knees.

"Oh, Ellen, Ellen," he whispered.

Ellen's heart was stifling her. She wanted to say, Kurt, you must not be so unhappy—you must not. But she could not speak at all. Involuntarily, her hand went out toward the bent head; hastily she withdrew it. Even the touch of her caressing hand was forbidden.

Panic-stricken, bewildered, Ellen sprang up and ran to her little cabin. She was running away, she knew that. But she did not dare remain there beside Kurt. Although she could not have told what she was afraid of, the instinct for flight was strong.

The next moment she was furious with herself. Why hadn't she stayed with Kurt, put her arms around him, when that was what she wanted more than anything else in the world?

A terrific din broke loose outside Ellen's cabin door, and she rushed out on deck. It was Paul Jean whanging on an old iron bell that had lost its clapper. Added to that, he was announcing lunch at his loudest.

"Come and get it! Come and get it!" He bellowed the words over and over. He had Jerry in tow with the hampers. The sailing of the vessel had been delegated to one of the crew.

"Squat where you are, everybody. We'll eat right here on deck. Snap it up, Jerry, me lad."

Ellen, hesitant at facing Kurt again, lost all her selfconsciousness immediately in the atmosphere of conviviality which Paul Jean created so naturally. Out of the hampers Jerry brought cold lobster, chicken, and turkey. There were fresh biscuits, baked before sun-up, no doubt, to be ready for them when they left so early in the morning. Jerry dashed back to the little galley to bring out steaming coffee and a tureen of melted butter. Setting an example, Paul Jean plunged big blobs of lobster into the butter and ate with a relish.

"Fall to, me hearties, eat up," the rollicking voice rang out. The high spirits of this big, generous man were infectious, and they all fell to with a will. But by the time they got to the luscious fruit, gathered on the estate, Paul Jean grew serious.

"Now I want to hear about your trip to Chicago, Kurt. And what's this I hear about Ellen siding with you about bettering working conditions for the miners and their families? Speak up, man."

Kurt launched into a description of the suggestions made by the superintendent of the mines.

"Well, he must know what's needed. He's a good man. Give him what he wants, Kurt." He turned to the girl.

"Now, Ellen, what is it you wish done for my miners? Going to turn my men into a bunch of sissies? Out with it, young lady!"

"Only things that will make them better workmen in the long run, not softies," Ellen protested earnestly. "Shorter hours, first, so that they can spend more time with their families. Playgrounds for the children next. I understand from Kurt that most of the settlements are isolated, so that the people cannot take advantage of the recreational centers in the cities. Next, but most important, I think, are health centers and welfare organizations."

"Well, well— *Well*."

Paul Jean got up and took a turn about the deck.

"You're the big boss, Mr. Hollister, to all these people. They have only what you allow them; their happiness, their very existence depends on you. I know you haven't neglected them, but there are so many fine programs for the betterment of workers—"

"Well—well, I'll be damned, Ellen." Paul Jean turned to Kurt, who was now standing beside him, listening to Ellen's plea. "Do you hear that, Kurt?"

He made a playful jab at Kurt's ribs. "She's all but calling me old-fashioned, and by the Great Horn Spoon, I like it."

He took Ellen's hand and whisked her over to a cushion. "Sit down here for a minute."

Kurt followed them.

"Listen to me, both of you. Ellen, here, has made me think, and when I think, I act. I'm going out to California to see the mines—and Ellen, you're going with me. When anyone can put up such a fight for people she hasn't even seen, it's high time she had a first-hand look at all this."

"But, Paul Jean, you haven't made that trip in over three years. Don't you think I should go? I could bring you back a report on just the things Ellen has mentioned."

"Thanks, Kurt. I never felt better in my life than I do right now. Old Doc Harrison is an old soandso."

His eyes were fixed on the horizon, and there was longing in them, as he added: "Kurt, my boy, I'm lonely for the old mines. I want to see them again. I really have a hankering for the old hills."

"Maybe I could go along with you," Kurt suggested.

"Nonsense. I won't have it. I've made the trip a hundred times. My mind's made up, and Ellen goes with me."

Kurt knew there was nothing more to be said.

"When would you figure on going?" he asked.

"Olivette's party is a week from tonight. I promised her I'd be there. Right after that, Kurt. Will you see about the reservations?"

"How about you, Ellen?" Kurt turned to her. "You'll go?"

"I'm delighted. I could learn so much. And it would help with the book, too."

Belying the words, her voice was wistful. She didn't want to go so far away from Kurt, now.

"I'm going to take the wheel again. You two come over here where I can talk to you."

Paul Jean stood for a moment, grinning at them, legs wide apart, arms stretched above his head. Ellen had never seen such sheer jubilation on a man's face. *That* was what he had been wanting all these months—to get out and see the mines again, and she had given him a legitimate excuse. He was a man to stir the imagination, and at this moment he looked young again, magnificent, even violent; no wonder men had followed him blindly, glad to do his bidding, back in the days when he was their active leader.

Kurt and Ellen stayed with him while Paul Jean talked. He was giving instructions to Kurt, who, of course, would have the full responsibility for the company while he was away. Ellen was glad not to have to talk, and she drifted a little apart, not paying much attention to what they were saying. She wanted to think about Kurt, clearly, if possible. She found she was more shaken by the scene with him earlier than she had realized.

She was happy. She wouldn't let herself think of what lay ahead. This was sufficient—life was beautiful just as it was. She dwelt on Kurt's generosity and patience toward Beatrice, who, it seemed to her, had made a mockery of their marriage. Ellen reminded herself that this was only surmise on her part, but it must have been what Kurt meant. Beatrice must be clinging to him, robbing him of the right to love and live normally, for obscure reasons of her own. She was taking advantage of Kurt's stark honesty; she knew he would put her wishes, as his wife, before his own.

Ellen could have followed what Paul Jean and Kurt were saying, but she made no effort to catch the words. Instead, she waited for Kurt's voice, and stood there enjoying the sound of it. It was enough to be within sound of the voice of the man she honored, trusted—and loved. She knew all at once that she loved Kurt—she reveled in the thought that she did love him.

Suddenly something was happening. All in a moment she was aware that Paul Jean was shouting at her. She could scarcely hear him above the wild wind howling around them.

"We're turning back, Ellen. We'll have to try to beat the storm. It's going to be a rip-roarer."

Ellen saw that the sky was growing inky black and that a terrific storm was tearing out of the northeast. Transfixed, she saw they were headed straight for what looked like a dark wall of water, which the next moment seemed to rear up and drop on the schooner like tons of watery darkness. Then she felt strong, firm hands guiding hers into the sleeves of one of the yellow slickers. Kurt was buttoning the corduroy collar under her chin. He put his face close to hers, to be heard.

"Don't be alarmed. We'll ride it out."

Swallowing up his voice, a mighty wave rose and dashed over the boat like a giant waterfall. Kurt put his arm around Ellen to steady her, and for a moment, as lightning blazed across the heavens, followed by the combined roar of the sea and the thunder, they clung together. Her hair was streaming out in the wind, and her eyes, fixed on his, were wide with apprehension; not for herself —for him.

He sheltered her with his body, braced against the cabin wall.

"You won't take chances—you'll be careful?" she whispered. He held her so close her lips moved against his cheek as she spoke. It was all they could do to keep their footing. Her eyes never left his face, and her upward gaze was unstudied, transparent. She had not meant to let him know she loved him. If she hadn't been so frightened for his safety this would not have happened.

It was not raining, but it might as well have been coming down in torrents, for the waves washing across the deck sent heavy spray shoulder-high. A weird half-light enveloped them. Between violent sweeps of wind, the air hung hot and thick. They could not see each other distinctly in the queer yellowish light, and only by clinging tightly together could they keep their balance. Kurt tilted her chin back gently, and, their faces dripping and splashed with cold salt water, their lips met.

"I could not help it," he said, huskily. Then, "Everything will be all right."

His arm around her, bent, fighting the wind at every step, they struggled to the cabin door, which was banging crazily back and forth. Kurt pushed Ellen inside.

"Latch the door. Put something against it—stay in there."

He was gone.

It had all happened in such a few seconds: the storm coming up raging, the terror that something might happen to Kurt, his kiss. Ellen sank down on the bunk, her drenched hair falling against her face.

Kurt had kissed her.

She sat there, bewildered. This should not have happened. Would she have to leave Hollister House? Would this make being under the same roof with Kurt intolerable? Then she remembered the trip to California. They'd be gone in a week, and be away for a month or six weeks. Time to think. She felt a surge of gratitude toward Paul Jean. She'd known him such a short time, and she owed so much to him.

Her excited thoughts ran on. Tremulous happiness began to take possession of her. She thought she was seeing bright lights, flashing back as from jewels—thousands of jewels. The air was fragrant, as if from unseen flowers. She felt a kind of lanquor steal over her. Finally she thought, Am I getting hysterical because of all that has happened? But after a minute, she told herself, No. I'm in love with Kurt. He loves me. That's all; that's what makes everything bright and warm and fragrant.

She was glad no word of love had actually been spoken. His kiss was vivid, all she needed to remember. After this, without Kurt, life for her would be meaningless.

A pounding began at her door and for a minute she feared it would go off its hinges. Paul Jean yelled, "We're still afloat, Ellen. Come on out."

Ellen looked out. The western sky was dyed with flaming, far-flung red and gold. They sailed away from it, for home.

The lights had not been turned on yet. As Ellen went up the stairs it was quite dark, and she kept her hand on the railing to be sure she wouldn't fall. She was trembling, too. She must pull herself together; this would never do.

When she got to the top step she thought there was one more to go, and she put her foot up where she thought it was, only to have it land on the very floor she was standing on.

"Ooo—o-h!" she gasped, involuntarily.

She was wearing her rubber-soled shoes, of course, and all the way up the stairs she hadn't made a sound. Now, at her exclamation, down at the end of the long gallery, against the dimly outlined square that was a window, did two figures move? Was that the tall figure of a man, in white, and a woman wearing something dark? The man was facing Ellen, and, although she wasn't quite sure, she thought he sprang back, while the woman, her arms still about his neck, tried to hold him. The man—Clyde? The woman—Beatrice? She wasn't sure of what she had seen. It was really very dark.

She stood still to get her bearings. And out of the gloom came a man, walking toward her, in white. It was Clyde. Thinking to escape, Ellen looked about, a little wildly.

She noticed it was raining again—a noisy, slashing downpour that made a terrific racket on the roof of the veranda below. Clyde was quite close now, smiling.

"Home? So early, Angel?"

Without meaning to, Ellen glanced past him to the window far down the gallery. Did a thin shape glide past the frame of the dim window? A second later, surely, even through the swish and drum of the rain outside, that was the sound of a door closing with an ill-tempered bang, somewhere in the distance.

"Let's have lights," Clyde said smoothly, snapping them on. "I came up here to see if the windows in the gallery were all closed. This rain came up so suddenly the servants couldn't get everywhere at once."

Ellen remained silent.

"When do I get to have a date with you, Beautiful? When is it my turn?" He added, insolently, "Or does everybody else come first?"

One moment Ellen was furious. The next she wasn't. What good would it do? The man was impudent, but impudence was part of his charm, and he knew it; it became him. He smiled his special flashing smile, calculated to smooth out any difficulty, Ellen surmised. She regarded him levelly.

"I've told you often enough I'm working; I'm not here to have fun. I wasn't having a date with anyone today, or any day for that matter. Today, as usual, was purely business." Suddenly, as she spoke, she realized how far from the truth that was; remembered Kurt's kiss. A warm flood of rose crept up under the tan of her skin.

The next moment Clyde's arms were around her, drawing her tightly against him. It was a rough embrace. The man didn't seem to care whether or not he hurt her. Ellen's wrought-up nerves snapped. She drew back her very excellent tennis wrist and landed a stinging blow on his cheek. The smile left Clyde's handsome face and he let her go.

"Did you have to do that?" he demanded.

When Ellen tried to pass him without speaking he barred her way.

"Did you?" he persisted.

Ellen, near tears, though she wouldn't have let him guess it, said, a slight pause between each word for emphasis:

"Shut up, Clyde Hollister!"

Clyde stepped aside immediately. But he said, his words and tone menacing, "You've made a mistake, my brave Angel."

Her head held high, she got past him and forced herself to walk with dignified tread down the hall. Gaining her room, she closed her door and locked it. How dared Clyde Hollister touch her! She realized sharply that she had been at fault that night when she had listened to him down by the sea wall. But he had seemed so sincere in his need for someone to confide in. Since then she had come upon that scene between him and Mary Gilly, and the girl had all but told her she was in love with him. Then, in the darkened gallery just a few minutes ago, was that Beatrice, Kurt's wife, in his arms, outlined against the window? If the woman were Beatrice, was she in love with this man, as well as Mary Gilly? Was Beatrice the real reason Clyde kept coming back to Hollister House? Ellen remembered that first night when she arrived; Beatrice had come in to greet the rest of the family on Clyde's arm. And the day she had crossed the terrace with him, Clyde had left her at the private stairway to Beatrice's apartment.

Later, after she'd crept into bed, she still felt as if her thoughts were being blown every which way by erratic winds. There were so many things she could not understand, things that were no concern of hers, really, unless they were to bring unhappiness to Kurt. If Kurt had come up the stairs when she did and found Beatrice at the window in the waning light embracing Clyde—Ellen shuddered at the thought. What kind of man was Clyde, anyway?

And Beatrice—she of the calm, straight brows, the drab monotone coloring—was it possible that strong emotion flamed under that glacial exterior —for someone not her husband? Or was Ellen just being too dramatic about Hollister House and all its occupants?

The wind outside had grown to frightening proportions. The rain slapped furiously against her balcony windows. Any other time Ellen would have gotten up to look at the fierce churning of the sea, but today she'd had enough of its wild strength and fury.

Strangely, the beat of the rain on the windows turned into the beating of jungle drums in her ears. Frenzied drums that never stopped. She moved her head restlessly. If she weren't so tired, she'd get up, try to escape the incessant sound, smash those drums.

She fell asleep, masses of her black hair tumbled on the pillow, her lips set, her hands balled into small, tight fists.

❖❖ 9 ❖❖

Ellen heard voices under her window. She raised herself on an elbow. It was morning; she must have slept after all. One voice rose above the others—Aunt Olivette's. Ellen glanced at her watch; only seven o'clock. She snatched her robe and ran to the window. Something must be wrong.

The wind last night had done great damage to the garden. In spots it looked as if it had been plowed under. Some of Aunt Olivette's priceless rosebushes had been uprooted, and many other plants had their poor blossoms dragging on the ground, submerged in pools of muddy water.

In the middle of all this was Aunt Olivette herself, shouting orders right and left to old Dominick and several other workmen. She was waving her silver-headed cane round and round, sometimes jabbing it into a new hole one of the men had dug to replant a bush, in an endeavor to speed up the work. The men were getting jabs, too, which they took as gracefully as could be expected.

Mercy, why is she driving them so furiously? Ellen thought.

She opened one of her windows and stepped out on the balcony. The moment she did, Aunt Olivette spied her.

"Ellen—Ellen—come on down here and help us. We've got to get these bushes back in the ground before she sun gets too hot. Oh, my poor darling garden," she went on wailing, turning her back on Ellen and starting after the gardeners again. Ellen dashed for her slacks and sweater.

Oh, this is so wonderful, she thought. To get out there and dig is just what I need, good hard work.

When she got out, Aunt Olivette was still bemoaning the havoc.

"We'll save you—every last one of you," she rambled on and on to the broken blossoms.

Ellen got down on her knees with the men and they all did their best. They dug holes; they replanted; and then they raked up broken branches and twigs. The physical exertion was what she wanted, and she was very glad to do something to help Aunt Olivette.

When all looked orderly once more and the sun really got hot, Aunt Olivette snatched off the kerchief she was wearing, and her white hair lay in ringlets close to the beautifully shaped head.

"Let's have breakfast out here," she said. "We'll wash our hands with the garden hose, there. I want to talk to you, anyway."

Laughing like a couple of children, they played the hose on their hands, and then Olivette sent one of the men to the house to tell Jeffers to bring coffee and toast.

"Got a cigarette?" Olivette asked, after they sank down gratefully in chairs set under a dense archway of wisteria vines. Ellen gave her a cigarette and lighted it for her. Olivette puffed away for a few minutes, then spoke softly.

"Draw a deep breath, Ellen, way down deep. Don't you dote on the smells of summer? The smell of the hot sun, new-cut grass, fresh-spaded earth— my garden, like the hundred and one fragrances of a giant bouquet?"

Olivette had put her head back on the cushion of her chair and closed her eyes. Her cane for once was still, laid across from one arm of the chair to the other in front of her.

"What memory-joggers scents can be." Olivette was speaking again. "I'm jogged right back to the day Kurt was married. My yellow lillies were in bloom, just as they are now. I sent wagonloads over to Beatrice; she wanted all yellow flowers. Her gown was yellow satin. That was eight years ago. I've hated the color ever since."

Ellen listened, fascinated. Why was Olivette telling her all this? It wasn't like her to speak of family matters.

Suddenly Olivette sat bolt upright, seized her cane, and leaned across to rap sharply on the arm of Ellen's chair. She didn't speak loudly, but Ellen was amazed at the vehemence of her next words— like the utterance of a slow anger that had built itself up over a long stretch of time.

"I hate Beatrice."

Ellen stared into the older woman's flashing eyes. She knew she was staring, but she couldn't help it.

"On account of the life she's led Kurt. I never liked her, even as a child, although she's the only child of my very best friend."

Jeffers was coming down the path with the coffee and toast and marmalade. Olivette waited until he had the things set out. As the man's straight back disappeared across the green lawn, she continued:

"I tried to the very hilt to like her, for her mother's sake. But, may the Lord forgive me, the child was plain repulsive to me. The day Kurt came home and told me they were engaged I couldn't believe it. If it had been *any* other girl. Paul Jean invited them to live here, and they came. Kurt was away a lot, in California at the mines and abroad; more and more as time went on. He seemed to want to get away. Beatrice entertained in her own apartment a great deal—cars going and coming at all hours. In my opinion most of them were men. We had to let one handsome gardener go; old Dominick said he was never available. Then there was always Clyde. . . . No one spoke to Kurt of these things. He and Beatrice just drifted away from each other. There never was anything in their marriage that could be built upon, that could endure; of that I am positive.

"Then a baby came, but it lived only a little while. From then on Beatrice said she was ill. She languished about when she was with the rest of the family. She either ignored Kurt or snapped at him. She was fretful and impatient with all of us. Finally she kept to her rooms for weeks at a time. But she wasn't alone by any means. She had many visitors. Her maids were forever leaving her. The general servants dreaded being assigned to work in her apartment.

"There was the period that lasted for years when she traveled all over this country and abroad for consultations with famous doctors. I suppose Kurt kept telling himself that it would pass, that she would get back to normal. Long since he had lived in his own rooms except when he received an invitation from Beatrice to visit her in her apartment. If she, in the early days, had ever trembled at the sound of his footstep, or grown weak at his touch, Kurt must gradually have come to accept the fact that that part of their life was done with forever. Personally, I doubt if there were any early raptures."

Suddenly Olivette got to her feet.

"That's Kurt's story—up to now." Her bright eyes clung to Ellen's for a moment. "Don't ask me why I told you—for I don't know."

She started off across the smooth lawn, Ellen by her side.

"I've grown fond of you, Ellen. I've got a gift for you. Come with me, I'll show you. Last time I went to my dressmaker's I got you a dress to wear at my music festival next Tuesday. We'll go to my rooms now and see how it looks on you."

A maid got the dress out of Olivette's closet. It was enveloped in cellophane and she laid it in the bed.

"I ordered it the day we had lunch in New York. Open it up, Ellen."

Ellen actually could not speak as she took the gown from the covering and held it up. It wasn't hanging on a hanger like an ordinary gown would have; it couldn't, because it didn't have any shoulder straps. The top of the bodice was clipped to a plastic hanger by two little plastic clothespins, and from there on it simply collapsed into hundreds of pleats of white chiffon.

"Blazing white, the designer calls it," Olivette told her. "I'm dying to see you in it. Help her with it, Della."

When the dress was on, Ellen looked into the full-length mirror to see a skin-tight bodice with layers of the chiffon twisted into a heart-shaped decolletage, from which the skirt drifted and floated as she walked. There was not an ornament of any kind—just yards and yards of gossamer floating about her.

"That's what I call simplicity by a master," Olivette said, walking around and around Ellen, lifting the soft stuff up and then dropping it to see it float back again.

"Not a jewel, not even one pearl, on those tawny shoulders of yours, Ellen. Isn't it marvelous the way it's wired to stay up without the straps?"

"Olivette, what can I say? Why did you give me such a gorgeous gown?"

"It pleases me to have you wear it, Ellen." She stood off for a moment, gazing at the picture the girl made. "If I had a daughter, Ellen, I would have wanted her to be and look just like you."

Olivette turned from Ellen as if to hide her emotion, as the girl instinctively held out her arms toward her.

"I wish you would take your gown up to Mary

Gilly for just one bit of alteration. The hem on the left side—it dips a trifle too much. Do that, will you, Ellen? Have her straighten it."

Ellen felt like crying, but she managed not to. Scarcely knowing she did it, she gathered up her slacks and sweater and went out of the room. When she got a little way along the hall, the library door burst open and Kurt dashed across the hall and up the stairs toward her, two at a time. He didn't see her the first few steps upward—then he glanced up and did. He stopped; he stood absolutely still, looking up at Ellen.

"Oh, Ellen," he whispered.

He came up the remaining steps.

"*Oh, Ellen. . . .*"

Her eyes were wide on his. His deep emotion kept her silent, too, as he looked at her.

"You—in that gown. . . ."

Then, making a supreme effort, he asked, trying to sound casual, "For Aunt Olivette's party?"

Ellen nodded, and making an effort, too, she held out the bedraggled slacks and sweater.

"These don't go with the gown, you know." Her smile glinted up at him. "I'm just carrying them around till I get used to the beautiful gown, so I'll know I'm me."

She turned from him gaily and ran away. She looked back when she reached the stairs leading up to the sewing room. Kurt was staring after her.

Ellen wasn't really surprised the afternoon a maid tapped on her door, as she was changing her dress for dinner, and told her that Mrs. Mabilla Marshall was downstairs.

"Send her up," said Ellen at once, feeling as if all the brightness had suddenly gone out of life. She put back on the shirtwaist frock she had just taken off. I'll have dinner with her here in my room, she decided. What else can I possibly do? Send word down to the housekeeper that we'll require another plate at the table? That Mr. Paul Jean's secretary's stepmother has arrived unexpectedly and must be entertained?

A moment later, Mabilla's orange hair was preceding her around the doorway in answer to Ellen's "Come in!" Mabilla was pretending to be overcome by the splendor of her surroundings.

"It really is you, Ellen," she cried now. "At first I was afraid to up and walk right in—this room is certainly grand."

"How are you?" asked Ellen, trying to keep the hostility out of her voice. "Did you write me that you were coming? I didn't get the letter."

"No, it was just a sudden impulse. You know me, always impulsive. Bob used to say I'd do something on the spur of the moment that I'd be sorry for some day."

Ellen winced at the reference to her father, and started to ask Mabilla to sit down. But her stepmother was already sprawled full length on the chaise longue.

"How is Aunt Margaret?" asked Ellen.

"Relieved to see me go," said Mabilla, rather frankly.

"But—" began Ellen.

"But nothing. I'm not hanging around that joint any longer."

"I thought you were going to help her use up some of her money." Ellen could not resist quoting Mabilla. The older woman was not in the least put out by the reminder.

"Your Aunt Margaret is a regular Tartar," she said, laughing gaily. "She had me waiting on those kids as if I'd been a nursemaid all my life. What's more, I was getting to like it. So I said to myself, 'Mabilla, this is no place for you. Before you know it you'll be wearing smocks, just like Aunt Margaret, and letting yourself go.' And I haven't reached the age when I can afford to do that!" She rambled on about the bus drivers and what she said to Bill and what Bill said to her, shrieking with laughter at her own sallies. Ellen interrupted to call the kitchen on the house telephone, asking that dinner for two be sent to her room. Mabilla's eyes narrowed as she listened, but she said nothing. During the meal, her high spirits returned and she chattered on as glibly as before.

Later Ellen told her that she had made arrangements to have her suitcase sent up to the room she was to occupy.

"Suitcase? I've got two trunks!" cried Mabilla. "Good night, darling. See you!" She went out of the door on this note of triumph, leaving Ellen despondent.

I'll just have to leave if she insists on staying, thought the girl. I can't expect my employer to accept my stepmother as a permanent guest.

For all her triumph over what she knew to be Ellen's inner distress at her arrival at Hollister House, Mabilla had changed her opinion of Ellen in the short time that had elapsed between dinner in Ellen's room and breakfast time the next morning. By questioning Ellen persistently, she had learned that there were two unmarried men in the house—fixtures, apparently—and her respect for Ellen had increased enormously.

Here was little Ellen, who had always seemed so unaware of her own advantages and the necessity for making the most of them, getting herself ensconced in a household where there were two of the world's most eligible men. At least, from what Ellen said, this Clyde Hollister seemed to have no wife about, and certainly Paul Jean, the elderly, handsome owner of all this luxury, was either a bachelor or a widower.

Mabilla was intrigued by the thought of Paul

Jean. In thinking of him, Mabilla, who had already given unaccustomed thought to Ellen, promptly forgot about her. She was not one to give undue attention to the problems of other people. It was Mabilla who interested her—Mabilla and her own problems, chief of which at the moment was: how was she to make herself "solid" at Hollister House? Paul Jean seemed to offer the ideal solution to this problem.

Mabilla dressed carefully for breakfast. She decided that she would wear her orchid satin lounging pajamas, and breakfast at ten. It seemed the likeliest hour for a meeting with Paul Jean. If he had arrived slightly earlier, he would still be in the breakfast room, if he had not yet come down, she would hang around until he did.

It was disappointing to find only a woman at the table when she entered the breakfast room, having asked the butler, who was sorting mail at a table in the hall, the way. Mabilla glanced at the woman at the table, noted briefly that she was apparently tall, almost gaunt, and had strange, cold eyes.

"I'm Mabilla," she trilled. "Ellen's mother."

"Ellen?" said the woman, as if she had never heard the name before.

"You know, Ellen Marshall, the new secretary to Mr. Paul Jean Hollister—or don't you live here?" Mabilla broke off to ask.

YOURS, WITH LOVE

"I live here," said the woman.

Mabilla was taken aback, for an instant, at her tone.

Then, "How lovely for you," she murmured. The woman did not answer, but Mabilla realized she must have trodden on the bell button, for a maid appeared suddenly at her side.

"Yes, Mrs. Hollister?" she said, inquiringly.

"More coffee, please."

As the maid left the room, Mabilla put out a hand. "You must forgive me, Mrs. Hollister. I didn't know."

Beatrice appeared not to notice the hand, and Mabilla pretended that she was reaching for a plum from the dish at the center of the table. The maid returned with the coffee and, going to the sideboard, began bringing dishes for Mabilla's inspection.

"That's a nice lot of electrical equipment," Mabilla observed appreciatively. "It does save a lot of time—leaves the maids free for other things, doesn't it?"

"What the maids do with their time is no concern of mine," said Beatrice.

"Oh." Mabilla was puzzled. "I get it—you've got a housekeeper."

"Must we continue to discuss the household machinery?" Beatrice burst out, irritably. She glanced toward the hallway, as if expecting someone momentarily. Mabilla had a distinct sense of having become invisible; certainly Mrs. Hollister never looked her way again, or even spoke. Mabilla, on her part, maintained a dignified silence.

Mabilla sat stirring a second cup of coffee after Beatrice had left the room. She was uncomfortable. She had made a tactical error and she knew it. The question now was, could she retrieve herself? Another wave of respect for Ellen's hitherto unsuspected abilities swept over her.

She has been living here and getting away with it, she marvelled, and I come down to breakfast the very first morning and put my foot in my mouth.

But Mabilla's despondent moods never lasted very long. She added a second lump of sugar to her coffee, after only a momentary hesitation, and got herself another piece of toast, spreading it thickly with marmalade. Clyde came into the room as she bit into it. She started guiltily when she noticed he was looking at her.

"I'm being good to myself, just this once," she defended herself. "I've been eating it dry right along."

" 'Live and let live' is my slogan," said Clyde, lightly. "Have you been breakfasting all by yourself?" He spoke casually over his shoulder, his back to her as he scanned the dishes on the serving table.

"No, Mrs. Kurt Hollister just left." She waited a moment, and when Clyde did not speak, added, with an attempt at gaiety, "You're later than I am."

Clyde came to the table with nothing but rolls. "I had my breakfast early. But I had to come back to the house, and lunch is still a long way off."

"Not that it's any business of mine!" Mabilla could not resist saying. "Coffee?"

"Please," said Clyde. "Did I sound as abrupt as all that?"

"I guess you didn't mean to snap my head off," said Mabilla generously, as she handed him his coffee. "Your mind was on something else. And to tell the truth, I wasn't the least bit interested in whether you were late or not."

Clyde smiled politely. "Maybe we'd better start over at the beginning. I'm Clyde Hollister."

"I'm Ellen's mother." Mabilla paused, expecting at least a flattering start of surprise. But Clyde only murmured, "Charmed."

"Stepmother," said Mabilla hastily.

"It must be pleasant for Ellen to have you here." Clyde's tones were even. Stuffed shirt, Mabilla thought, viciously.

"Have you come quite a distance?" Clyde continued.

"Quite." Mabilla's voice was taking on a measured quality of its own. "Westchester."

Clyde laughed and got up. "You must excuse me. I've got to get back on the job." He had taken only a sip from his coffee cup.

Mabilla eyed his retreating back with disfavor. I've seen plenty of his type, she told herself, without bothering to decide what "type" Clyde Hollister was. She didn't like him. Mabilla never liked any man who didn't fall for her, as she put it, on sight. She wasn't the kind who would work at getting a man's attention. She didn't have to.

In spite of these heartening reflections, she had a slight suspicion that she was not, so far, a success in her role of girl-stepmother. The orchid lounging pajamas had failed to create the effect she had intended.

She went upstairs to change to something more nearly approximating Mrs. Kurt Hollister's simple frock. When she came down again, she was wearing a demure, dull-blue cotton dress with a little eton jacket, comforting herself with the thought that the jacket could be whipped off, if the occasion seemed to be right for it, and that the dress beneath was not only sleeveless, but backless.

It occurred to her now that it was entirely within her rights to find Ellen, wherever she was keeping herself, and show some concern for the kind of work she was doing. After all, she was the girl's stepmother. Armed with this high-minded purpose, Mabilla asked a passing maid where the library was.

Outside the designated door, Mabilla, after a

second's consideration, slipped off her jacket, draped it negligently over her shoulders, adjusted her face to a broad smile, thought better of it and toned her expression down to a bright look, and knocked on the panel of the half-open door. There was no response, and no sound whatever from within. Mabilla pushed the door open further. The room was empty.

She tapped at several closed doors and looked into rooms that were unoccupied, until she caught sight of one of the maids staring at her from the end of the hall. Thereupon she went abruptly out on the terrace, through the open French windows of a small sitting room, and presently discovered Olivette's rose garden.

But, though she lingered until she was afraid her nose was getting sunburned, no one appeared, and Mabilla, tiring of her pose of rapturous appreciation, which was being wasted, walked on along a path that brought her, at long last, to the corner of the garden where Paul Jean and Ellen were working. Paul Jean was dictating in his usual booming voice. At the first slight pause, Mabilla, emerging from the shrubbery behind him, spoke up.

"There you are!" she cried. "I was beginning to feel like Goldilocks in the bears' house. I couldn't find a soul!"

Ellen's head, bent over her notebook, snapped up suddenly, and Paul Jean, getting to his feet with reluctance, dropped a handful of loose notes. The breeze seized upon them and they started to dance across the paving stones toward the flower borders.

"Oh, I made you do that!" Mabilla, running with little steps, stooped for one of the sheets at the same moment that Paul Jean stooped too. Their heads collided sharply, with an audible thump. Paul Jean straightened up, then bowed to Mabilla.

"Permit *me*, madam," he said.

"No, I must help you," cried Mabilla. "It was all my fault." She rushed around, chasing the flying sheets of paper, her laughter tinkling gaily. She was making such a gay flurry that the two great Danes, coming out of the little wood where they had been for a walk with Flossie, decided to join in the fun, and one of them, barking wildly, snapped at the one paper that Mabilla had been able to rescue. She pulled it back, just as the dog's jaws closed on it. She yanked, the dog tugged.

"Let go," shrieked Flossie, taking in the catastrophe instantly. "Let go, you—you dope!" to Mabilla. At that moment the dog, twisting his head rapidly from side to side, tore the sheet out of Mabilla's grasp and chewed on it vigorously. He was still chewing when Flossie, rapping him sharply on his nose with the palm of her hand, made him drop it. But it was now useless pulp.

"Darling Paul Jean! Was it very important?"

Flossie cast herself into Paul Jean's arms. He patted her hair, but set her gently aside.

"It doesn't matter. I had just read it and I can dictate it now, approximately, from memory—if Ellen and I could be permitted to go on with our work."

"He's throwing us out," Flossie told Mabilla cheerfully. "Better step on it. Here Wisty! Here Maggy!" She was off along the path to the rose garden, her hair flying behind her as she tried to keep up with the racing dogs.

Mabilla stood for an uncertain moment. Ellen, acutely aware of the awkwardness of the situation, felt that she was remiss in not introducing Paul Jean to her stepmother. But how could she, at this point, say anything so anticlimatic as, This is . . . While she was struggling with courtesy to Mabilla and awareness of her employer's annoyance, Mabilla settled the matter by departing, retreating hurriedly the way she had come.

❖❖ 10 ❖❖

The night of Olivette's music festival Ellen hesitated a long time before she could force herself to go downstairs. The whole affair was so much more—"glittering" was the only word that occurred to her—than anything she had ever attended. From her windows she could see the grounds, lit up as if it were midday, by the great spotlights turned on the terraces and gardens, and a steady stream of cars that had been arriving for the last half-hour.

Mabilla had flounced off to New York the day before, telling Ellen to expect her when she saw her. Now, waiting in her room for the proper moment to go down, the girl was grateful that her stepmother had gone. She could not remember ever having been grateful to Mabilla before.

At last, with a final reassuring look into the mirror, and a smile of sheer happiness over the beauty of the white chiffon dress, she made her way down the front stairs. She was wearing her hair parted down the middle as usual, and it fell in soft lustrous black waves below her shoulders.

The entire first floor was thronged with people. Ellen had checked over a partial list of the guests with Olivette the day before, and although she did not know one from the other, she did know that many important people were there, especially musicians. Surprisingly enough, there were many young people; home for the summer vacations, Ellen supposed.

Ellen hurried toward the ballroom. She was anxious to see it for the first time. It was opened only for special occasions like this.

Most of the flowers had come in the late afternoon and Ellen had not seen them properly arranged until now. They were massed everywhere. The scene ran mad with color and the air was laden with perfume. She glanced in as she passed the state dining room, and saw the tables ready for the buffet supper. Tables had been placed around three sides of the room, and they were three tiers high. Ellen got an impression of gigantic swans that looked as if they had been made of colored glass, or it might be gelatine, poised on the top tiers. All around them and on the tiers below, delicacies that you'd have to eat to recognize had been formed into shapes of flowers, birds, and ships.

Was there ever, anywhere, such a party before? Ellen asked herself.

Finally, she was at the wide open doors of the ballroom, and by adroit side-stepping she got herself inside, where she could stand out of the way for a moment to watch the dazzling scene. The room itself was the most beautiful she'd ever seen. Two stories high, plate-glass windows to the ceiling, all thrown open—it was regal. All the windows were covered with drapes of heavy white net, from ceiling to floor, hanging from full gathers at the top. The slight breeze that stirred them made the whole room look as if it were set in softly drifting snow. Again, as in the gallery on the second floor, there were great crystal chandeliers from which lights beamed and winked through the glass prisms.

The orchestra was playing Strauss music; the musicians wore white suits with gold buttons and gold braid. Ellen saw, way down on the far side, Olivette and Paul Jean, flanked by Beatrice in a red gown, a matching scarf flung over her drab hair, and Kurt, still in the receiving line. But at this moment there was a fanfare from the musicians, the crowd fell silent, and the conductor turned and faced them.

"You will kindly take your places for the grand march," he announced.

The center of the floor began to clear at once, and as it did, Ellen saw Olivette, her hand on Paul Jean's arm, step forward. Other couples quickly fell into place behind them, and started to march down the center of the shining floor.

The next moment she felt each arm gripped in a firm hand. Just this side of alarm, she glanced up quickly, first at one owner of a hand, then the other. Both turned out to be very tall, slender young men, eyes meeting over her head, who gave every appearance of being about to take pokes at each other.

"Ken, you're a dog," the brown-haired one addressed the other man, pulling Ellen possessively toward him.

"Go hang upside down—you're batty," the very blond one expostulated with considerable heat.

"I saw her first."

"You're a dog—you did no such thing," repeated the brown-haired one.

Ellen looked up into first one earnest, handsome face, then the other. She had never seen either of them before.

"Boys—boys! May I get in on this?" she managed to make herself heard.

They both apologized, without either one releasing her.

"Suppose I have the march with one of you, and the first dance with the other?" she suggested placatingly.

"Oh, no, you don't," from the blond one, as the other started to tuck her hand under his arm.

"You're a dog—" It was starting all over again.

"Tell you what," Ellen raised her own voice a little. "One of you walk on each side, then." She noticed people were beginning to smile a bit as they passed by.

With grim faces, heads high, the young men stepped into line beside her.

"I'm Ken Dunbar," the blond informed her.

"I'm Tom Dunbar," the brown-haired one offered.

Giving names looks like a return to reason, thought Ellen.

"Will you come to our first football game this fall?" Ken demanded. "I mean, with me?"

"If I ask her, she can't go with you. I'm a senior—remember?" from Tom.

"Just a moment, boys. Don't you want to know who I am?" Ellen asked.

"Oh, that," said Ken. Tom announced with finality, "You're my dream-cake."

They marched along with swinging steps, neither one letting go the grip on her arm.

"Thank you so much, but I cannot go with either of you to the football game. I am Mr. Hollister's secretary, and my time is all taken up with his work. He's writing a book. I'm Ellen Marshall."

She added her name a bit lamely, as it was so evident that it was of no importance to either of them.

At a turn in the serpentine formation of the marchers, Ellen caught a glimpse of Kurt, the red-clad Beatrice on his arm, stiff and unyielding.

Then the couples, at Paul Jean's direction, formed lines four abreast—then six, and so on. Later, after another fanfare, a waltz began, and the couples started dancing. Ellen would have liked to stand and watch them glide over the satiny floor, but the blond one had outskirmished the other Dunbar by some technicality which Ellen didn't quite get, so she found herself whirling along, round and round, in what must be the latest collegiate conception of the waltz. Three turns was the limit before the other boy cut in, one simply following while she did her turn with his brother. Ellen tried to find Kurt in the crowd, but couldn't. This went on for the first three dances, without letup, until she gasped:

"Gentlemen, may I be excused," and before either could get that by now familiar grip on her arm, she fled blindly to the terrace.

Little tables dotted the terrace, all the way to the pool. If people sat down at any of the tables, a waiter would appear out of the bright night with a bucket of champagne and cigarette trays. Even the three-quarter moon seemed bent on adding its own particular beauty to the scene. It sailed against a deep blue velvet sky, trimmed with golden star sequins.

Finally Ellen turned to look at the flowers and the extravagant tropical green shrubs and rare plants Olivette managed to make grow. She took a few steps toward a tall group arrangement. There, in the fragrant darkness, a man was sitting on a bench looking at her. He threw his cigarette away, came slowly over, and took both her hands.

"Oh, my darling. . . ."

"Kurt!"

"I've been watching you dance."

"I didn't see you."

"I sat here and looked at you."

A quick step was coming along the flagstone path toward them. Instinctively, they both turned and walked forward, side by side.

"My dance, I believe, Ellen."

Clyde held out his crooked elbow with exaggerated courtesy. She hadn't seen him since she had slapped him that night of the storm.

"Ellen is sitting this one out with me," Kurt said, his tone brittle.

"May the lady be permitted to decide?" Clyde's handsome dark face was taut, his tone rude.

"The lady has decided," Kurt said through tight

YOURS, WITH LOVE

lips. The next instant his left fist shot out and clipped Clyde on the jaw. The man staggered back and fell onto the bench.

Still sitting there, Clyde said, "We won't brawl here, dear cousin. But remember, I owe you one."

Very few people had noticed, and those who did see the blow either moved away or discreetly kept on talking among themselves. However, suddenly something was happening. Light feet, almost running, raced along the flagstones; a red fury flung itself among them—Beatrice. Her red scarf had become loosened and was trailing down off one shoulder, dragging with it a coil of her hair to which a hairpin still clung. Her eyes were dark pin-points of hate, her voice just this side of screaming—at Ellen.

"What are you doing here at this ball? You don't belong. How dare you come here as a guest? Answer me—answer me, you—you—"

Beatrice made a quick swoop and grasped Ellen's bare shoulders with clawing fingers. Kurt and Clyde each sprang forward and wrenched the woman's hands away.

"Are you quite mad, Beatrice?" Kurt demanded. She turned on him.

"You'd like that, wouldn't you? Wouldn't you? You'd like that very much."

Beatrice had lowered her voice, but her rage hadn't subsided; it was cold, frightening. Ellen didn't know whether the woman was furious with her for talking to Kurt or to Clyde.

"Oh, stop it—stop it," Clyde said impatiently, as if suddenly he had taken great aversion to the whole scene. "Come and dance with me," he ordered Beatrice. "But first fix that thing on your head, or take it off—and control yourself."

Ellen thought for a moment that Kurt would strike him again, but suddenly the whole place swarmed with people. Paul Jean came storming down upon them, Flossie dangling on his arm.

"Ellen, you're to rumba with me. Maybe you think I can't. Flossie, here, has been showing me. I'm damned good—damned if I'm not. Didn't know it was in me."

She danced with Paul Jean, who was very good indeed at the rumba. After that, men came up to Paul Jean and she was introduced to one after another. She danced on and on. The men kept tapping her partner on the shoulder and someone else would cut in. She simply couldn't remember all their names.

"Olivette is going to sing in a few minutes," one of them said. "Shall we go down and hear her?"

"Oh, yes—please," Ellen answered.

Down by the lily pond a platform had been put up, and chairs had been arranged for crowds of people who were flocking to hear the singing.

YOURS, WITH LOVE

Olivette was already there, in a gown of silver pailletes. She sang twice; then she was joined by other singers. They did arias from operas, ballads. Indeed the night was filled with music; the setting was indescribably beautiful.

Presently Ellen saw Paul Jean coming toward her.

"Just had word from the airways, Ellen. Our reservations are okay for tomorrow. We'll leave from LaGuardia Field."

His eyes were dancing in anticipation. The thought struck Ellen again—he wants to make this trip more than anything else in the world; he actually loves those historic old mines.

She looked about for Kurt. Would he say goodbye tonight? Wouldn't she see him again before she left? She would be gone a long time. A strange dread took possession of her. What if she never saw him again! Was it enough that she had stirred him deeply, that she had been close to him for a little while, that she had seen warmth and eagerness in his eyes at the sight of her?

Rebelliously, she put away the thought of life without him—Kurt *was* life to her. It simply couldn't be that their loving each other would turn into something sweet but useless—just a memory. Would she have to strike out, try to build a new world for herself where Kurt would never be? At the thought of it, she felt lost.

"Ellen." It was Paul Jean. "Can you be ready to leave by twelve tomorrow? Kurt will drive us in to New York."

Ellen woke up the next morning unhappy, even angry with the whole world, an unusual mood for her. Why had she fallen in love with Kurt? Was she to bring more trouble into his life? The thought was unbearable. She had coffee very early, alone. When the time came for her to go down to the car, using all the will power she possessed, she tried to crush every tender emotion from her heart. That would be best for Kurt, she had decided.

Paul Jean was already in the great hall, his arm around Olivette's waist. She was pleading with him to be careful.

"How many times have I made this selfsame trip, old girl?" he protested. Then, with a bearlike hug, he was off, down the steps. Kurt was at the wheel, ready to start. He waved at Olivette, Paul Jean lifted Ellen almost bodily into the back seat and, with surprising agility for such a big man, flung himself in beside Kurt.

"Be good to yourself," he shouted to Olivette, who, waving a dainty bit of lace handkerchief, was making a brave show of gay leave-taking. It occurred to Ellen for the first time that Olivette was worried about Paul Jean's taking this long trip. Also she remembered, with a mental jolt, that it was she herself who had given Paul Jean an excuse for going to the old mines again. A dull, aching feeling engulfed her. Blindly, almost with bitterness, the thought rushed at her: The two people I care most for in all the world, Kurt and Paul Jean—will I bring them both unhappiness, even tragedy?

"All set?" It was Kurt speaking to her. He had turned around from the wheel, his arm on the back of the seat, his eyes deep on hers.

"Yes," she answered, "all set."

For the space of what might have been a minute—an hour, eternity—their eyes held. Ellen was hearing again his words as he took her hands last night.

Oh, my darling . . .

It was all there again in the silence between them, it was just as if he were saying the words again. In that moment Ellen entered another world with him—his world and hers, warm, and fragrant. Paul Jean, the servants, and Olivette, the big house, all lost reality.

"Back to the mines, boys!" It was a mighty shout from Paul Jean. The servants stepped out of the way. Kurt swung back to the wheel.

"Step on it, let 'er roll! California bound at last," jubilated Paul Jean, grinning back at Ellen.

She saluted smartly. "Right you are, sir," she responded, getting as much life into her voice as she could.

After that, as they spun along, there was no need for Ellen to try to join in the conversation. Paul Jean and Kurt were deep in business details almost immediately. Ellen was grateful. Her thoughts were confused, emotional, excited. She found herself remembering Kurt's kiss on the schooner the afternoon of the storm—the salt taste of the cold sea water as it sprayed their faces. She was surprised at the violence of her love for Kurt. Last night, thinking to spare him in the dreadful situation in which they found themselves, she had tried desperately to repress her feeling for him. She tried hard now.

You're acting like a silly schoolgirl. You're stupid, or you would have found some way to avoid all this happening.

Deliberately, she hurled insults at herself, trying to blot out the memory of moments with Kurt. She didn't succeed too well. Still she kept at it savagely, building up a firm resolve to stop remembering his strong grip of her hands, as if he never wanted to let them go, the sound of his voice, husky when he said her name, his eyes on hers.

Shivering a little there in the back seat, Ellen knew she would fail in her resolution. When Kurt had looked at her, back there before they started, the uncontrollable flame had blazed up again. It would do no good for her to go on resisting. She knew now that, from the first moment she saw Kurt, she had known he was the one man she could ever love.

As they neared LaGuardia Field strange sounds filled the air. Twin motors idling on the taxi strip kept up a steady undertone. There was the deep-throated zoom of a homeward bound skyliner circling the airport.

"Oh, this is exciting," Ellen exclaimed, getting out of the car and slipping a hand under Kurt's elbow. Enthusiastically, she tucked her other hand under Paul Jean's arm. "Let me hold on tight. I want to keep my feet on the ground; I feel as if I'm flying already."

Paul Jean patted her hand; Kurt smiled down at her.

They stood watching as a plane glided smoothly over the airport boundary. The silvery craft leveled over the macadam runway and its wheels touched the ground.

"Safe home," whispered Ellen.

"Happy landing," Kurt said, so low only Ellen could hear. He pressed her arm close and put his other hand over hers.

Paul Jean kept saying, at regular intervals, "This is the way to travel—the only way, damn it all."

Presently, Kurt was shaking hands with Paul

Jean in farewell. Then he was holding her hand, tight.

"I want to go with you," he said grimly.

Ellen could not speak.

There was no more time.

The beautiful ship took off smoothly, and they were sailing through a drift of clouds. Every minute took Ellen farther and farther away from Kurt. The waters of the East River and Long Island Sound, Bowery Bay and Flushing Bay, glinted in the sun and disappeared. When would she see them again? When would she see Kurt?

"We'll be in California tomorrow, Ellen. That's pretty wonderful. We're living in one hell of a fine world."

Paul Jean was enjoying himself hugely.

Ellen looked out at the great white blobs of cotton clouds that took on fascinating shapes. The airplane was flying so smoothly that it was an effort to remember that she was in a plane at all. She felt herself suspended somewhere between heaven and earth. Later she marveled at the sunset colors, blazing away off on the rim of the world. Later still, she watched, enchanted, the brilliant stars thickly spiking the sky.

❖❖ 11 ❖❖

They were met at the airport by the superintendent of the mines. Other officials were there, too, to welcome Paul Jean.

Paul Jean was impatient to get out to the mining district. He confided to Ellen that when they got out to the region which was the locale of the early part of his book, they would "give everyone the slip." Ellen knew by now that what Paul Jean wanted to do, he usually did.

They started for the open country. The superintendent and a young engineer named Edwards went along with them in the automobile. Later, when the going got rough, they were to ride horseback.

Ellen learned a great deal about what had happened to gold in the past few years. She listened, sometimes taking notes on such facts as Paul Jean decided should go into his book. In regions where hydraulic mining was permitted, she saw where whole hills had been washed away by water pressure, so that the gold could be extracted from the dirt with the least effort. They went through valley lands where gold dredges had done a big job in extracting gold.

"There are thousands of places where men can still pan for placer gold and get small flakes," Paul Jean said.

Then one day it was thought advisable to leave their car and ride horseback, as it would be easier to get close to the mines.

This is it, thought Ellen. There will be some excuse for Paul Jean to leave the others. He'll ride out where's it's lonely and dangerous.

The very next day there was an excuse. The superintendent got word that something had gone wrong back over the route they had come, and instead of Paul Jean and Ellen going with him, they were to stay overnight in a small community just ahead. The superintendent said he would get back to them by noon.

"A half-day's rest will do you both good," he told Paul Jean and Ellen. "You two just stay here and wait, and Edwards and I will go back. It's nothing serious. I'll see you again in no time at all."

YOURS, WITH LOVE 167

Their horses had no more than carefully picked their way down the rough, narrow dirt road, and the two men had turned to wave good-bye, than Paul Jean turned gleefully to Ellen.

"Of all the luck! Mount and ride, young lady. I'll show you where the Hollister mines got started."

"Is it far? What will you tell the superintendent and Edwards?"

"It's a few miles from here. We can make it in no time. The others can follow."

"How will they know where we've gone?"

"I'll leave a note. I know this country like a book—it's like old times."

Ellen tried her best to dissuade him, but nothing she could say would stop him. They were soon on their way.

Although Ellen knew that Paul Jean was a splendid horseman, from the first she had felt uneasy about the horses they had been given to ride. Paul Jean's was a magnificent deep-bay pony, full of fire and high spirits. He even tried to dislodge his rider at the very beginning, but Paul Jean loved that, and soon had him under control with apparent ease. Ellen's horse was almost jet black, a smaller animal, but young and spirited, too. Both horses knew they were being handled by strangers.

"You can gentle her, Ellen. We're well mounted," Paul Jean had said.

They started off at a brisk canter. But they didn't

keep it up very long, for almost at once the road got more difficult. Ellen was obsessed with the dreadful doubt that they should have waited for the others. She said so.

"Oh, they wouldn't want to ride out to the old mine; think it a waste of time. But I want to see it, and I want to show it to you," Paul Jean announced flatly.

The earth was wrapped in golden sunshine, and the tranquility under the shadowy pines lulled Ellen's fears a little. The ceaseless murmur in the trees high over their heads as a warm breeze drifted through them was soothing, too. Finally Ellen spoke.

"It's so calm—so limitless. Do you think the first settlers saw it this way?"

"Just so, maybe. Except when the Indians were whooping it up."

"How you would have liked to have a go at it back there when it was so wild?" Ellen laughed.

Her understanding of him put Paul Jean in high good humor again.

"You're darned tootin' I would," he exclaimed. Then he started reminiscing, and Ellen loved to listen.

As Paul Jean talked, she kept watching the road anxiously again, for the trees gave the effect of beginning to push in on them as the road grew narrower and more rugged. She glanced up and away into the distance. Nearby, and as far she could see, there were hills, big and small. There was a lot of lofty rock formation, jagged in outline, that stabbed the sky. Hills and flat land, where there was any, were covered with big and little pine trees—pine trees everywhere.

Paul Jean talked on—and they rode on. The road was so rough now the horses had to go slowly, carefully picking their footing. Fervently, Ellen wished the other two men would catch up with them. It was dangerous, she felt sure now, to be riding out alone like this. There wasn't any real reason why they should, either. It seemed very silly to be taking such chances. Suppose something should happen—an accident! They were so far away from everyone. Suddenly Paul Jean shouted and pointed with his riding crop:

"There—that's it, Ellen! See those two steep hills over to the north? There's a deep ravine between them, and that's where our first and richest mine was discovered. Let's go!"

Apprehensively, Ellen noticed that the sun had suddenly disappeared. Paul Jean wasn't disturbed in the least.

"Don't mind if it rains a little," he called back. "There used to be a neat little cabin right along here somewhere. Generations of the Tubbs family lived in it. We'll take shelter there if we have to."

But Ellen's growing dread was accentuated by

thick, dark clouds that were heaping themselves on the tops of the trees, shutting out the light completely. A weird, desolate moaning emanated from the writhing branches above, for the wind was really blowing a gale now. Birds made short, unquiet flights. Then big splatters of rain hit down hard through the trees for several minutes, followed by the downpour.

Paul Jean wheeled his horse and came back to Ellen. He leaned forward to make himself heard above the uproar.

"Over there. See the cabin? You can just make it out, the other side of that brook. We'll make a dash for it."

In two minutes they were drenched to the skin, but they urged their horses on. The road was full of boulders and loose stones that were very slippery. Lightning jagged across the wild scene and the thunder deafened Ellen. They would have to cross the swirling brook to reach the cabin. She saw Paul Jean point with his riding crop across a meadow, so she headed for it, her horse making a mad dash over the level stretch. Paul Jean was a few yards behind her.

How the accident happened Ellen never knew. One moment they were both making good headway, considering the heavy going, when a deadly fork of lightning neatly spiked a tree stump just back to her right. Involuntarily she turned her head to see what had happened. She saw Paul Jean's horse rear and swerve, and Paul Jean was thrown to the ground.

Ellen turned her horse and waited, expecting to see Paul Jean get up, tearing mad. A tumble from a horse wasn't so bad. But Paul Jean didn't get up. He was lying on the wet ground, very still. Ellen galloped back, swung down, and threw herself on her knees beside him.

"Mr. Hollister—Mr. Hollister," she gasped. She was so frightened now she could scarcely make a sound. His face was gray-looking and all at once blood began to trickle across the sharp stone beside his head. That was it; his head had struck the stone. He was unconscious. Ellen cradled his head in her arms, tears streaming down her face.

"Are you all right? Please say you're all right," she begged the silent lips. Finally, she saw it was no use. She sank back, terrified. She tore off her coat and made a cushion for his head.

"He's dead," she sobbed. "He's dead—and I'm to blame. He wouldn't be out here if it weren't for me. If he's dead I want to die too."

Something made her realize that she was screaming the words, there in that abandoned meadow, rain pouring down on both of them. Another realization came to her: I've got to get help, somehow. I've got to get a doctor.

Ellen ran to her horse, mounted, and dashed

toward the rushing waters of the brook, across which she could see the cabin dimly. Maybe, as Paul Jean said, there will be someone in that log cabin.

She was only partly across the brook when she saw two figures emerging from the cabin door. They saw her, for they mounted their horses and galloped toward her. As they came closer she saw that one was a young man, the other a much older man, both obviously miners. The young man raised his arm in greeting.

"In trouble?" he yelled.

"Will you see what you can do for Mr. Hollister? His horse threw him."

"Mr. Hollister?" the young man cried. He turned and sped to the prone figure of Paul Jean. Ellen rode after him and so did the older, little gray-haired man. The young man rose after a swift examination.

"He's not dead. Concussion, probably, and his leg is broken."

"Thank God, he's alive," Ellen whispered.

"It's a darned good thing we have the wagon here with my equipment. You two stay here and I'll take both horses and hitch them up and get back as soon as I can with the wagon. We can put Mr. Hollister in it and get to that next little town—Blue Valley. They have a telegraph station and we can get an ambulance to come out." He dragged off the hip-length waterproof cape he was wearing and handed it to the old man.

"Here, fix this over him as best as you can."

The next moment he was gone.

Paul Jean wouldn't have made this trip if I hadn't started talking about bettering the mining conditions, Ellen thought dazedly. It was more than she could bear, and she felt like weeping, but managed not to. Even as she gulped back the tears she saw the team of horses drawing an ordinary flat wagon splash into the brook and across it. Then it was only a few moments before she heard the young man directing the lifting of Paul Jean into it.

Ellen climbed into the wagon, sat on the floor, and took Paul Jean's head in her lap. The young miner rolled up canvas to support the injured man's back and leg, and drew the waterproof cape over him. Ellen hunched her shoulders forward to shield Paul Jean's face from the rain. The old man sat on the floor, too, steadying Paul Jean with his hands. The tortuous journey began and continued in silence, except for the creaking and unavoidable bumping of the wagon on the rough road, for what seemed to Ellen a very long time. Finally, the old miner said to her kindly:

"We ought to make Blue Valley in less than an hour. It will be better when we get an ambulance from there."

It wasn't hours they'd been traveling, then; only minutes, Ellen knew. She glanced from habit at her wrist, but her watch was gone.

Some time later she noticed that miraculously the rain was dwindling off; soon the sun burst on them in unclouded glory.

Just as if nothing had happened, Ellen thought.

In the bright sun it was all a little less grim. And then, in the far distance, they made out two horsemen riding toward them. It proved to be the superintendent and Edwards, racing to meet them. They stopped, and soon the two men drew up beside the pitiful group. Ellen explained.

"What? You can't mean that. Paul Jean thrown from a horse? Why—the horse hasn't been born that could throw him."

"It was the storm. The horse reared."

To Ellen it didn't seem that the ride would ever end, as they were forced to make their way slowly. She kept her place beside Paul Jean on the floor of the wagon, trying her utmost to allay the jouncing along the miserable road. The young miner did a wonderful job of driving, desperately trying to avoid the bad spots. But at one turn they found they had to ford the brook again. As the horses splashed through the muddy water and struggled nobly to keep their footing, Ellen was sure the wagon would overturn. The superintendent and Edwards sloshed along beside them, and whenever the wagon showed a tendency to swerve up on either side, they gave it a mighty yank down, as they leaned far out from their saddles. The horses heaved themselves out and up the opposite bank. No one spoke.

They reached Blue Valley at last. The ambulance was called and Ellen telegraphed to Kurt.

Dr. Harrison, who took charge of Paul Jean at the hospital, was one of his lifelong friends, Ellen was told. Now there would be more waiting while it was found out how badly he had been hurt. Ellen was feeling nothing, really. She was suffering with shock caused by horror, apprehension, and exhaustion. She was trembling with cold, and Dr. Harrison, when he came out to them, sitting miserably in the waiting room, glanced at her sharply.

"You're all concerned about Mr. Hollister I know," he said, "but you cannot help him by remaining here. And you, young lady," he turned to Ellen, "need a sedative. Every one of you go and get out of those wet clothes," he ordered. "We have to behave sensibly."

"Please, Dr. Harrison," Ellen said. "I don't want a sedative. May I come back after I've changed into dry clothes?"

"Well—all right," the doctor agreed grudgingly.

Obediently, Ellen went to the hotel, changed, and sent for hot coffee. When she got back the others were there ahead of her, and the girl at the reception desk handed her a telegram. It was from Kurt. As she saw his name at the bottom of the message, she felt that he was there beside her, reassuring her, after all these dreadful hours. His message read:

Be brave for us both. Flying. Be with you soon.

Her blood raced warm again, for the first time since the accident. Kurt would know what to do; he would do everything possible and with a firm hand.

Be brave for us both.

Ellen went over by the window and sat down. She closed her eyes to think of those words. Only two things mattered now—how seriously Paul Jean was hurt and seeing Kurt again. It was curious that the whole world otherwise was actually dimmed out for her.

A door was flung open and Dr. Harrison came in smiling.

"Good news for you folks. Paul Jean has fully regained consciousness. It was quite a crack that sharp stone gave his head, but I don't think there's anything to worry about. He has a severe back contusion, and, as you already know, his leg is broken. All we need to make him as good as new is a little time; nothing that time and care won't cure."

The doctor walked over to Ellen.

"Paul Jean wants to see you, Miss Marshall. Will you kindly come with me? But talk to him for only a few minutes."

They walked up some stairs covered with soft rubber, almost like thick carpet. They went to a floor some stories above in a small private elevator, then along another corridor. In a few minutes the doctor looked back at Ellen and nodded reassuringly, then stopped before a door and tapped lightly on it. It was opened at once by a nurse. Now Ellen could see Paul Jean, in bed, a bandage around his head and his leg in a cast. He was tearing mad.

"Will you look at the hell of a fix I've got everyone in, Ellen? Thrown from a horse—me! Why, a horse wouldn't dare!"

The break in his leg was between the ankle and the knee, and Paul Jean insisted on keeping the cast in full view on top of the bed covering.

"See that blasted thing, Ellen?" he demanded, shaking a balled-up fist at the cast. "I'm grounded by this dratted leg—got to lie here flat on my back and sweat it out."

"That'll be all of that, Paul," Dr. Harrison interposed. "You gave me your word you'd be quiet."

"Yes, I did for a fact," poor, helpless Paul Jean agreed. "And I will." He turned to Ellen.

"I only wanted to see for myself if you were all right. My good friend here would lie to me about the weather if he thought he could shut me up that way." But he winked at Dr. Harrison. "You all right, Ellen?"

"Of course I am, Mr. Hollister. Just worried to death about you."

"You can see for yourself, I'm absolutely tiptop. No more worry now, Ellen. This will just delay the book a little, that's all."

He was tiring, Ellen could see. At a nod from the doctor she said good-bye to Paul Jean.

When Ellen reached her hotel she found another wire from Kurt, telling her when his plane was expected to get in, and that he would go directly to the hospital. Then the telegram continued:

> *Thanks for standing by with Paul Jean. All my love.*
>
> *Kurt.*

There it was, in words. Kurt loved her. He was telling her so across the miles between them.

Ellen threw herself down on the bed, the open telegram clasped in both hands. She lay there motionless a little while. Then, unbelieving, she raised the telegram to read it again and again. She had thought that perhaps some day Kurt would tell her he loved her, if by some miracle it would be right for him to do so. But she never thought it would be like this. She wondered, What does he

YOURS, WITH LOVE

mean to do? Answers did present themselves, but on second thought every one of them seemed unreasonable.

At last she got up and walked slowly about the room. Was there going to be some way out, after all, because they loved each other so? Was all this darkness with which she had seemed to be surrounded for the last few days to be dispelled? Was there something that would make it right for them to be together—to ride along country roads, walk on the beach under a bright moon, laugh together over silly things just because they were happy, because they belonged to each other? She dare not dream any more. She whispered:

"You will be with me tomorrow, dearest. I want to understand. Please help me."

The next day, Ellen and all the others waited for Kurt in the small reception room attached to Dr. Harrison's office. Ellen stood at the window and saw his taxi drive up. As he sprang out and took the steps two at a time her pulse did crazy things. He looked taller, browner than she remembered, and purposeful. He would know what to do about everything. Dr. Harrison went out to meet him and then the other men crowded about. Ellen stood back so he could talk to them. But his eyes sought her out and he came over to her with quick steps.

"Ellen—Ellen, you're not hurt? You're all right?"

"I'm really all right, Kurt."

Kurt looked searchingly into her face a moment longer, then went back to Dr. Harrison.

"Will Paul Jean see me now?"

"He's all but pulling the hospital down about our ears waiting for you," the doctor told him. Kurt smiled for the first time; he looked over at Ellen.

"Will you go to your hotel and wait for me?" he asked her. "I'll phone you in about an hour."

"I'll wait," Ellen said.

It was two hours later when her telephone rang. She told Kurt to come up. It had started to rain again, and she had had a fire built in the fireplace, but it was almost out now. Try as she would she could not make the dreary hotel room look inviting.

The door flew open—Kurt strode in. Ellen was standing by the mantelpiece, hanging on to it with one hand to steady herself; her heart raced. Kurt threw a bouquet of red roses, dripping raindrops, on the table, and came to her swiftly. With the utmost gentleness he drew her to a shabby settee by the dying fire.

"Oh, my darling." He no more than breathed the words. His arms held her close and he kissed her.

"I've been afraid, Kurt. I was alone."

"And my place is by your side. You'll never be alone again."

YOURS, WITH LOVE 181

He drew her to her feet, placed her arms around his neck, his about her waist. Her eyes were wide on his.

"Ellen, my life depends on your answer. Do you love me?"

"I love you, Kurt."

"Then, my darling, everything is going to be all right. I'll make everything right. Say you believe me."

Ellen nodded her head in assent. It was hard to speak.

"Say it—oh, my darling, say it," he demanded. "Tell me you know everything will turn out right for you and me."

"Whatever you do, dearest, will be right."

That was what he wanted to hear. Kurt tightened his arms around her, as if defying any fate cruel enough to try to wrest her from him. After a while he led her back to the settee.

"I have only these precious moments with you, Ellen. I have to see some people tonight about chartering a plane to take us home. I'll come back here as soon as arrangements have been made. We'll drive out and have supper somewhere. And tomorrow the superintendent wants me to go out to the mines for a few days. But I'll be back for you tonight the moment I can break away. Will you wait?"

"Always," Ellen told him, her voice unsteady.

He held her by her slender shoulders and looked down at her as if he couldn't let her go. Then he kissed her. The door closed after him, and Ellen was alone. But the room was warm now, and filled with soft light. Kurt loved her—he would be back in a little while.

They drove out along a glistening highway, the trees arching above still dripping from the last shower.

"Sit close to me, Ellen." Kurt put out his arm and pulled her over against him, so that their bodies touched, side by side.

"This is fantastically sweet."

His expression was very serious; he looked down at her as if he couldn't quite believe that she was there. She smiled a little, dreamily. It didn't seem very real to her, either, but she wanted to believe it.

The weather was capricious. All at once there was a starry sky above them, big, soft, blurry stars, and the night was beautiful and still. When they stopped for the next light, Kurt leaned toward her, strangely subdued.

"You said you loved me, Ellen, darling. Tell me again."

"I love you, Kurt, completely."

He listened eagerly, watching the starlight shining in her eyes.

"The magic of it," he murmured, as if wondering how this could be so.

They caught sight of a suburban night spot, with lights blinking invitingly, at the top of a gentle hill. He looked at her and she nodded. The inn was an old mansion, converted into an eating place; it was painted white and had double verandas running around two sides of the building. The proprietor beamed at them and led them to a table on the upper veranda. He lighted a shaded lamp on the table. Ellen listened to Kurt's voice as he ordered cocktails.

When the cocktails came he touched the rim of his glass to hers. They smiled into each other's eyes. These few captured moments were all they had as yet. They would make them last as long as they could. Soft music came from nearby.

When they had had their coffee and Kurt had lighted her cigarette for her, he put out his hand toward her, and tightly grasped her hand in his.

"I must tell you something, darling."

"Yes, Kurt?"

"I'm going to ask Beatrice for a divorce when we get back."

Ellen's fingers trembled in his firm clasp and grew icy, even while his love was warm around her heart. Her eyes were earnest on his. She felt suddenly bewildered and her voice sounded stifled as she gasped:

"Oh, Kurt—oh, no!"

"Ellen, my darling, don't tremble so. Don't be frightened. I couldn't bear it if you were frightened, or hurt."

Ellen managed a smile. "I'm not frightened," she said. "It was only—just as first."

Kurt got up suddenly, came around the table, and sat beside her.

"I can't bear to be so far away from you, even for a moment. I never felt like this before about anyone. When that plane left New York, taking you away from me, it was intolerable, the loneliness, all at once. I want you near me so I can hear you speak, so I can look at you, always. Say you know what I'm trying to say, darling."

He was pleading for understanding, boyishly.

"I do know, Kurt. I—I've been lonely, too."

After a pause Kurt went on, almost as if thinking aloud. "I'm not going to talk about my marriage. It was a mistake for us to marry at all. It isn't as if Beatrice cared. I think she knew that we weren't right for each other before I did." He hesitated, then went on.

"Almost from the first we sensed something was wrong. We tried to make it work, but we were in a difficult situation. We didn't want to do anything until we were sure. Our families had always been close. We had the same friends. We were considerate and decent toward each other. But the

YOURS, WITH LOVE

time slipped by—months, then years. Little by little Beatrice changed; became finally as you see her now. These last few years we have been almost strangers to each other."

Ellen's eyes were lustrous with unshed tears.

"And then, Ellen, I saw you."

"When did you first know you loved me?" she whispered.

"That first day," Kurt answered.

Happiness held them both fast for a little while. No words were needed. They got up and walked over to the veranda rail where they could look down into the tops of the trees. The moon was dodging in and out among the clouds, and moonlight striking through the myriad festoons of raindrops clinging to the leaves turned the world into a glittering place.

"When the routine things are attended to, I'll come for you, darling."

"You'll come—for me?" It was a question.

"Yes, I'll come for you—so we can be married."

He took her in his arms and kissed her. As he held her, he murmured, "I love—and I am loved."

❖❖ 12 ❖❖

When Paul Jean was out of danger, Kurt took two days to look after the firm's interests, going off on trips with the mine superintendent.

"I'm tempted to take you along," he said once to Ellen.

"Oh no. Don't ask me. I must stay with Paul Jean."

In fact, Ellen remained with Paul Jean almost constantly during the next few days, bringing him magazines, reading to him, taking notes whenever he had a stray thought for the book. At night, as she stood in the doorway of his room waving goodbye, she felt a lump in her throat. He looked so helpless, big, hearty man that he was, lying there all alone on the narrow white cot.

At times, when she was alone, Ellen wondered, unhappily, what would be the outcome of Kurt's talk with Beatrice. Suppose she refused to give him a divorce? Suppose she was as unbalanced as she sometimes seemed, and would try to revenge herself on Kurt? Thoughts like these brought on a dull ache in her heart. Without Kurt she grew confused, accused herself of having brought about all this. But always, and almost defiantly, she would tell herself in the end that she and Kurt were meant for each other. I'm glad I met him. If I should never see him again, I'm glad I met him. There will never be any other man in the world for me.

The night Kurt returned, Ellen was sitting by Paul Jean's bedside. This was a different Paul Jean. The big, boisterous man still tried hard to shout and browbeat everyone within reach, but the strain had begun to tell on him.

Kurt took a hand of each and sat down on the bed.

"Both of you kids listen," he said. "Everything's ready for the take-off tomorrow at two. I was able to charter a plane."

"Good work, my boy. I can always depend on you." Paul Jean smiled and made a brave attempt at his old brusque manner.

"Now, the two of you get the hell out of here, so I can get some sleep for the trip tomorrow." He rang for his nurse to show he meant it. "Go dancing, you two," he growled.

"Dress up for me, Ellen darling," Kurt said softly, on the way back to the hotel. "Did you bring anything?"

"Just a plain black dress."

"One that shows your shoulders, so that every other man in the room will want to kill me when he sees you with me?"

"A little," Ellen laughed.

When Kurt called to her, he pinned two enormous reddish orchids to her frock. "My Ellen," he whispered.

At the night club they sat near the dance floor, amidst a whirl of dancing couples, while the music beat an insistent rhythm into their consciousness.

"Ellen," he said, "we're together again."

In a wild rush of feeling, she wanted to tell him that it wasn't enough, that she wanted to throw herself into his arms and be held close, that she wanted to show that she loved him. But she couldn't tell him that. Her eyes told him when she looked at him.

"Let's dance," he said abruptly, disregarding the cocktails the waiter had just brought.

"An excuse to hold you in my arms," he said, his lips close to her cheek. "Look up at me, Ellen.

Your eyes are a dark night-blue tonight, and there are stars in them."

Her smile slanted up at him. His blond head bent down so that he could touch her cheek to his.

The music ended and they went back to their table. The atmosphere of gay companionship subtly colored this hour that was theirs, so that it became not an hour but infinity.

The sense of being alone in a lovely world, forever, remained with them all the way home. Kurt left her at the door of the elevator in her hotel, but it did not seem to Ellen as if he had really gone. His presence was with her still—in the remembered nearness of him, the warm tones of his voice. But most of all in the words he had whispered just before they said good night:

"We have added a few more captive moments to those that were already ours," he said.

Ellen liked that. She liked to think of any moments shared with Kurt as belonging to them for all time.

The plane trip home was swift, although it didn't seem so to any of them. Paul Jean wanted to get home, that was all there was to it.

When they reached Hollister House at last, rolling up the driveway in the private ambulance Kurt had ordered, it seemed to Ellen as if Olivette were standing where they had left her, smiling at them from the doorway, with the servants grouped about her. But she knew that they must feel as she did about Paul Jean, that it was almost unbelievable that he should be lying helpless, unable to stamp around and shout. Olivette, she thought, must have schooled herself rigidly, for she rushed down to the stretcher, threw her arms around Paul Jean and demanded in her velvet voice:

"Who's a sissy now? Shame on you."

But as Paul Jean was carried upstairs, Ellen saw Olivette standing with her hands white and taut on the silver head of her cane, while slow tears dropped unheeded. She dashed them away in another moment and marched firmly up the stairs after them. Paul Jean's rooms had been rearranged so as to accommodate considerable hospital equipment. His back injury, still extremely painful, required heat therapy, for one thing, and there were various other devices installed to lessen his suffering and hasten his recovery.

Olivette insisted that Ellen had saved Paul Jean's life, and would accept no other explanation. On the very night of their return home she came to Ellen's room and asked for particulars of the accident. Olivette listened without comment until she had finished, then came over and put her arms around the girl.

"Ellen, you saved him. You saved my brother. You stood by."

YOURS, WITH LOVE 191

The girl protested again that the miners had managed the rescue.

"Oh, of course I understand they accomplished a few mechanics of the rescue. They saved Paul Jean to the extent of calling aid, but you saved him with your heart. There's a difference, Ellen, and it's a difference I value. What are you bawling about?"

"You're so kind," said Ellen, laughing in spite of her tears. "I never knew anyone so kind."

She was to discover that Olivette could be firm, too. As they walked along the gallery past Paul Jean's rooms, they heard light footsteps coming down the stairs that led to Beatrice's apartment. Beatrice herself came into view a moment later— a changed Beatrice, wearing a very short, very smart cocoa-colored frock that magically changed her drabness and thinness into a semblance of youth. Her hair, which Ellen had always seen twisted on top of her head, was hanging free in a shoulder-length bob. She came on down the stairs, turned her back on Ellen, and said to Olivette:

"Going in to say good night to Paul Jean."

"Oh, no, you're not!" retorted Olivette. "Is it possible you don't realize how seriously my brother is hurt? He can't be disturbed, certainly not without the doctor's permission."

"I was going to ask the doctor." Beatrice spoke in a sullen tone, but Ellen had the impression that she would have preferred to scream at Olivette. The older woman stood stonily silent, however, and Beatrice, wilting after an instant, spun around and went up the stairs again. They could hear her running up after she was out of sight at the turn, and Ellen remembered, with surprise, the pensive, trailing gait which Beatrice had always affected.

"Going in to say good night to Paul Jean indeed," said Olivette, indignantly. "Maybe she thinks I didn't notice myself how good-looking that young doctor of Paul Jean's is! I never stooped to watching our Beatrice before, though I've had my suspicions, but in view of her sudden change of personality, I think I'll keep my eyes open."

Ellen could scarcely believe Olivette's implication about Beatrice, which she had hinted at before. She felt a pang of sympathy for Kurt, and remembered, with admiration for his restraint, that he had made no accusations against Beatrice to her.

The house seemed more vast than ever, with Paul Jean confined to his suite, Olivette almost constantly near him, and Flossie away, still on the crest of a wave of marital tranquility. Clyde she saw only fleetingly.

Since Paul Jean's accident, there had been no more dinners in the big dining hall. Ellen either ate in her room or dined with Olivette in her apartment, at her invitation. Of Kurt she had seen very little; when he was at home he was in Paul Jean's rooms, and he frequently stayed in New York overnight, so that she had scarcely spoken to him for several days when one afternoon a maid brought her a note.

It was a guarded message from Kurt:

Meet me tonight at eight-thirty, at Paul Jean's big chair. Important.

There was no signature, but Ellen knew Kurt's handwriting well by now, having seen it on many documents belonging to Paul Jean. And she understood perfectly that he meant Paul Jean's big chair down in the garden, where he had dictated so much of the books.

"I had to see you, my darling." Kurt came out of the shadows to meet her as she reached the appointed place. He led her to the chair and sat her down in it, sitting down himself on the broad arm, where he could look down at her.

"Paul Jean isn't going to be able to continue with his book for a few weeks, Ellen," he began, without preliminary. "The doctors forbid him to make any effort whatsoever, mental as well as physical."

"I could go b-back to New York," stammered Ellen, taken aback by his words. "I could stay there until he was able to work again."

"No. No, Ellen. Don't leave us, just when you're needed here. Olivette likes to have you about—she told me so. But, Ellen, I have to go away. Not forever," he hastened to add, seeing the stricken look that crossed her face. "It will be for about a week. I have to make a trip to our southern branch. There's no way of putting it off any longer."

He paced up and down. "I only wish I could take you with me, Ellen!" he burst out. "I dread leaving you here without me."

"Why?" asked Ellen. "I have a great deal of transcribing to do. I still have a lot of notes I took on your uncle's book to type for him. I won't have time to get into mischief."

"You know I didn't mean that," Kurt cried, before he saw that she was laughing at him. They laughed together, and then, becoming serious again, he found a footstool and drew it up close to her chair.

"I'll leave you in Olivette's care, then. But, oh, my darling, don't leave me. Stay where I can find you."

"I want to stay near you," said Ellen.

"I'm not going to speak to Beatrice about—a divorce"—he hesitated over the word—"until I return from this trip. It might make the house uncomfortable, even unsafe for you. When I'm here and can take care of you, I'll tell her."

He stopped, and Ellen saw that his face looked drawn.

"I love you, Kurt," she whispered, impulsively. "If it has to be silently, secretly, for no matter how long, I will go on loving you."

He drew her to her feet and they walked along the wood path in the gathering dusk. They talked softly and when they came to a rustic bench, encircling a giant tree, they sat down and Kurt drew her close. A sliver of a new moon swung over the tree tops; the first stars were hesitant, pale gleams against the darkening sky. Night birds, abroad too late, chirped apologetically, then, with a hurrying whir of wings, settled down somewhere overhead.

A frog sounded loud by the distant lily pool; another answered.

Kurt's lips were against the dark head on his breast as he murmured, "No other man could love you half so well, my Ellen." Then, "Kiss me," he said.

Under the leafy arch of the trees, half hidden in the shadows, with the moonlight just touching their faces, a spell held them, making them one with the silence that now enveloped them; but in their hearts was tumult.

When they returned to the house, they met Olivette, all smiles.

"Paul Jean asked me to sing to him tonight," she cried. "He's really getting better. Kurt, I'll have my small piano moved up there, and I can sing to him whenever he wishes."

"I'm so glad," Ellen told her.

"I told you so," Kurt said. "You can't keep old Paul Jean down." He put his arm around his aunt's waist, and she clung to him for a minute.

"There, I'll snap out of it," she said then, whirling around like a girl. "Have you two had dinner?"

They admitted they hadn't.

"Then come with me. I skipped dinner too, and I'm having a snack in my apartment. . . ."

In the morning, Kurt had left before Ellen came downstairs. As soon as she could establish herself in the library, she started transcribing her notes furiously. She couldn't think of Kurt while she was working, and she felt that she could not endure a whole week without seeing him, if she had time to think.

The days crawled by. Olivette dropped in every afternoon to suggest to Ellen, as if it had just popped into her head, that they have tea together in the garden. It was Olivette who chose where the tea table was to be set. Sometimes she'd want to sit close to the long, narrow beds of flowers that glowed scarlet in the blaze of the setting sun, and sometimes she would choose one of her still-blooming rose hedges.

YOURS, WITH LOVE

"You've made this ordeal bearable for me, Ellen," she said once.

On an evening toward the end of the week, Ellen, going over her small wardrobe, discovered that several of her dresses were in need of repairs. Wondering if Mary Gilly were still in the house, she took two of the dresses over her arm and made her way to the sewing room. Mary was not there and Ellen remembered she had not seen her for a long time. Probably she was at home, in her little cottage, where she lived with her picturesque old grandfather.

It would soon be dark, and a small belt of woods lay between the big house and the cottage; but who would be on the grounds except those who belonged to the estate? Ellen had no fear of the dark, anyway. She started off gaily. The moon would be coming up soon and it would be bright enough, she reflected, as she moved along a moss-grown footpath, as soft as carpet to walk on, and as noiseless.

Not far from the cottage there was a summer-house set cunningly in the woods. Her footsteps turned toward it, almost without volition. She wanted to think about Kurt, and the summerhouse offered an invitation she could not resist. As she sat down she shook the dresses she had been carrying, to shake off the dew. The mist from the sea swept across gardens and woods at Hollister House almost as soon as the sun went down, these close-to-autumn evenings. Ellen laughed outright when a small shower of drops fell from her hair too.

How fresh everything smelled, and how still it was. Back of the summerhouse the trees massed together, dark and brooding. The silence was a bit frightening, but Ellen liked it. She could see the cottage from where she sat, and as she looked at it, the door suddenly opened and Mary Gilly stood outlined against the light from the hall. She had a cape thrown over a light dress, and she stood motionless, in an attitude of waiting, her eyes toward the wood.

Ellen jumped up. She must get back along the path before Mary's visitor made his appearance. The girl thought she was alone; it would be embarrassing to be sitting here, to watch the meeting. But, dismayed, she found she was too late. Mary had come quickly down the steps, was already coming along the footpath under the trees. Perhaps her ear had already caught the sound of steps which Ellen had not noticed.

Ellen, out of sight, shrank back on the seat. While she sat there, unable to decide what to do, Mary passed the summerhouse and, a few steps along the way Ellen had come, stood and waited for a man who came toward her slowly, as if reluctant to meet her at all. Ellen saw the girl lift

YOURS, WITH LOVE 199

a hand as if to brush away tears; then she saw the man.

It was Clyde.

He came close to Mary before he stopped, his hands in the pockets of his sports jacket. Mary, with what sounded to Ellen like a soft little moan, twined her arms tight about his neck, as if no power on earth could loosen them. Clyde stood without touching her for a few seconds, then seized her arms, and jerked them roughly from his neck. Mary, now crying brokenly, slid down until she knelt on the damp moss, her arms about his knees. Ellen started up again, thought better of it, and sank back on the seat. How could she let them know she was here now? It would be dreadful for both of them.

Clyde seized Mary roughly by one arm and dragged her to her feet.

"In the name of heaven, you little fool, why did you send for me? To make another damned scene?"

Mary stood silent, her white face turned imploringly up to him.

"You're not the first girl who's ever had a baby. And you don't have to go through with it. My last word to you is to take this. Here—" he pushed something into her hand. "And this card"—he felt in his pocket and brought out a bit of white cardboard—"has the name of the doctor I told you about. And stop this infernal fuss. You're getting on my nerves, and I warn you, that isn't good."

Ellen leaned against the back of the seat, chilled and so stunned she could not think. Again she looked wildly around for a means of escape. There was none. If she tried to get away, they would certainly hear her, even if they didn't see her, and to betray her presence would only humiliate Mary further. She could only sit motionless and watch through the screening leaves while Mary lifted her hand and let the bills Clyde had forced upon her drift slowly to the ground. The man had turned and was walking slowly away.

Mary Gilly's voice rose to a thin scream. "I'll kill myself, Clyde—I mean it."

The handsome, evil face looked back at her.

"There's a lot of deep water in these parts. That's as good a way as any."

Mary remained where he had left her, looking after the tall, straight figure moving insolently along the path. Clyde looked back once more.

"That's all rot about suicide. All your kind of girls try it on some man. Stop being a damned fool and get to that doctor."

He was gone, lost in the shadows.

Mary Gilly started to walk back toward the cottage, slowly, as if every step were bringing her nearer to some terrible fate. Ellen sat on, dully, horrified at the scene that had taken place before her eyes. Was there anything she could do to help Mary? A slight breeze came up and blew the bills playfully this way and that; Ellen's gaze, riveted to the spot where Mary had stood, saw them stirring and fluttering. She sat perfectly motionless, trying desperately to decide what to do. When she finally rose, the woods around her were quite dark. She had made up her mind; she would talk to Mary, try to get her to promise not to do anything rash, but to wait until she, Ellen, could find some way of helping her.

With her dresses in one hand and her courage in the other, she thought ruefully to herself, she made her way to the cottage. There was no light to be seen now, so she called:

"Mary! Mary Gilly—you have a visitor."

There was no answer for a time, but Ellen, sure that the girl must be inside, kept on calling. Finally, a light went on and Mary came to the door.

"Oh, it's you," she said, rudely.

Ellen's heart sank. "May I come in?" she asked.

Without answering, Mary stepped back and opened the door a little wider.

"Did you meet anyone in the woods on the way over?" she asked, suspiciously.

"No, I didn't," Ellen answered truthfully. She hadn't *met* anyone.

The girl had turned sulky. "Well," she said, "couldn't your dresses wait until morning?"

"I wanted a walk," explained Ellen. "I just thought I'd leave them here with you. I'm in no hurry for them."

Mary had stepped back so that the light fell on her face.

"Why Mary," said Ellen, "you've been crying. Can I help?"

"Why don't you ask me if I've been crying about Clyde?" The girl came over close to Ellen. "Go ahead—ask me. That's all you people at the big house have to do, pry into other people's affairs. Maybe you want him for yourself, Miss Marshall. Now, as you don't seem to be leaving this house, I will."

She dashed past Ellen, her face furious, and disappeared into the night. Slowly Ellen followed her and drew the door shut after her. She went home through the woods, across the terrace, her mind busy with the events she had witnessed.

Mary was so distraught she didn't know what she was doing or saying. That was clear. But what should she do about it? Tell Olivette? She hated to do that. But, if the girl were so overwrought that she was intending to commit suicide, shouldn't she try to stop her?

She met Olivette leaving Paul Jean's rooms, and the older woman invited her to have a bite of supper with her. Ellen went along, drank a cup of chocolate with Olivette, and tried to think of a way to introduce the subject uppermost in her mind. Finally she said, flatly:

"I saw Mary Gilly this evening. She's so upset! She said something about suicide."

"Oh, she's probably had a quarrel with some boy in the village. That sort of girl likes to dramatize herself, I'm afraid."

Ellen couldn't very well say: Not a boy in the village, but your nephew Clyde. She's going to have his baby.

"Aunt Olivette," she asked abruptly, "would you mind very much if I left you for a while? I'd like to see my Aunt Margaret in Westchester."

"You're homesick for some of your own family. And you've been through such a lot with Paul Jean. I think it would be the best thing in the world for you. But when you're rested, promise you'll come back to us."

"I want to. So much." Ellen smiled as she left the room, but once outside she stood still for a moment, her hand pressed against her eyelids. Her eyes smarted, as if from tears she had not shed.

Ellen walked slowly to her room. She went to her desk and started to write a letter to Kurt—one she didn't want to write. It wasn't going to be easy. She didn't quite know herself what was driving her away from Hollister House. Would she be breaking her word to Kurt by going, when he had begged her to be here when he returned from his trip?

No—not exactly. She had only told him, "I want to stay."

But now this wild desire for flight had full possession of her, and she couldn't fight against it. How blind she had been to her own situation. The scene between Mary Gilly and Clyde obsessed her, no matter how hotly she protested to herself, It isn't the same—it isn't—it can't be.

But the terrible disquiet remained. Had she and Kurt any right to their love, any more than Clyde and Mary Gilly had?

She started to write again. The pen behaved badly. It stuck in the paper and poked a tiny hole; then there was a blot. She took a fresh sheet of paper:

> *I will try not to make this a love letter, dearest Kurt. I must be sensible and strong. Try to understand. I am going away for a little while, to be by myself, so I can think about us. Suddenly I know that my love might hurt you. That must not be. Let me think.*

As she put a few things into a bag to take with her, the scene between Mary and Clyde kept coming before her.

Poor Mary. She must have lived in a trance, at first, thinking that such a man as Clyde could love her—he, all things wonderful, all perfection, so handsome.

Such thoughts, and constant wondering if Mary really meant what she had screamed to Clyde about committing suicide, made Ellen feel sick. Her throat was parched.

When I mentioned suicide to Olivette she didn't seem worried.

But then Olivette didn't know what Ellen knew. It would be impossible for Ellen to tell her what she had heard.

❖❖ 13 ❖❖

Early the next morning Ellen carried her bag downstairs. She found Olivette waiting to say good-bye. They had coffee together and had time to look at some of Olivette's beautiful flowers before the station wagon that was to take Ellen to the train got there. As they stood admiring a rosebush full of late bright pink half-blown blooms, a messenger came speeding up the drive on a motorcycle.

"S'cuse me, ma'am—you Miss Hollister?"

Olivette said, "Yes, I am."

"Sorry ma'am—I have bad news—very bad. The body of a young girl was found on the beach a few miles below here. We know who she is, that is, who she was—that is, one of our men did—that is, does—"

"For mercy's sake, get on with it, man. Who was the girl?"

"Mary Gilly, ma'am. We brought her back here to the cottage where she lived, with her grandfather, they say."

"Oh, I'm very sorry, very sorry indeed to hear that."

Olivette's hands gripped the silver-handled cane until the skin pulled across the knuckles. Ellen couldn't look any further than the older woman's hands, clutching the cane for control. She couldn't meet her eyes; not just yet. She couldn't say to her. It was Clyde, Aunt Olivette—Clyde who killed Mary.

The station wagon drove up.

"I'll stay with you."

"No, Ellen. Clyde is here. He will arrange everything. No, you must go away, and as quickly as possible."

Ellen's hands flew to press against her lips, as if to press back those words that must not be spoken, about Clyde and Mary.

"Besides, Ellen, there will be newspaper people and unpleasantness—sure to be in these cases. I can handle the reporters. I'm used to them. But I want you out of it. Go to your Aunt Margaret just as you planned. That's what Kurt would want."

A realization that Aunt Olivette knew that Kurt loved her came so forcefully over Ellen that she stood still, not able to move at all. Aunt Olivette, without another word, took her arm and almost pushed her into the car. Dry-eyed, throat tightening, Ellen sat slumped against the back of the seat and was driven to the station. After that she sat through the ride on the Long Island train to New York, took a taxi to Grand Central station, then found herself on the train to Westchester—almost without conscious effort.

Against her best efforts not to dwell on the tragedy and what led up to it, Ellen's thoughts tormented her. Poor little wild-hearted Mary Gilly. What a weight of pain she must have endured as the realization came that Clyde did not love her— had never loved her at all—and then, finally, the knowledge that he despised her.

It was a stifling day. The train was hot. When Ellen glanced out of the window, she saw that a yellowish, sultry haze had settled over everything. Menacing storm clouds had banked themselves into dark mountains over in the west; thunder mumbled in the distance.

She dropped her head back against the back of the seat and closed her eyes. Thoughts began drumming in her head again.

I'm leaving you, Kurt, because I love you so much—so very much.

YOURS, WITH LOVE

A whisper of denial escaped through her parted lips:

I don't want to leave you, dearest, but we can't have our love turn into something we'd both hate. Only, please—please come and find me and bring me back.

She knew her thinking was incoherent, but she could not stop the rushing thoughts.

"What shall I do? Oh, what shall I do?" she murmured.

"What say?"

It was the man in the seat beside her. He thought she was speaking to him.

Ellen did not answer him. She turned her face to the window and sat so he would see only her beautifully tailored dark blue shoulder if he looked her way.

She couldn't stop thinking about Mary, either. Had she in that last hour walked out slowly into the water, in one of the many still little coves that dented the shore line? The water would be quiet there. Did she walk out wearily, step by step—farther—farther, always? The water would reach her knees. A few more lagging steps; it would reach around the slim waist—there was still time to turn back. But no voice had called to her; there was no living thing to see. Night rested gently on the dark water; all was hushed.

If I go on thinking things this way I'll die of

it. Ellen pressed both hands to her temples. Weakly she thought, If some time would only go by. After a week or two, maybe things will get settled in my mind, all by themselves.

When she got off the train she remembered that Aunt Margaret always liked to have the New York paper. Perhaps she took it regularly, but, just to make sure, Ellen bought one. Without even thinking of reading it, as she rode along in the taxi her eyes fell on some headlines:

> Young girl on the fabulous Hollister estate on Long Island commits suicide—motive unknown. Body found in waters nearby. Last person to see her alive believed to be beautiful Ellen Marshall, secretary to Paul Jean Hollister. Miss Marshall cannot be located.

White-faced, Ellen sank back on the seat, away from the windows. Oh, if she could ever just get to Aunt Margaret's!

"Please—please drive faster," she implored.

Through the edge of the window she caught the first glimpse of the old brick dwelling where she'd spent so many vacations as a little girl. She still shrank back, but the sight of the well known house revived her a little. Aunt Margaret had been her tower of strength back there through her childish troubles; she would not fail her now. But how could she ever begin the recital of all the things that had happened in the last few months? Oh, what a mess she'd made of it all; Mabilla herself couldn't have used less judgment.

As the car swung into the drive she wondered if Aunt Margaret would be surprised to see her. She didn't have long to wait to find out, for in the distance, there on the lawn, she caught sight of her, waving wildly in welcome. She was running now, lightly as a girl. She clasped Ellen in a vigorous hug.

"Elly," she stormed, making believe she was upset. "Elly, baby, for heaven's sake get in there to that phone and call the Long Island operator. Get a Miss Hollister. I've got the number written down for you. She's kept the wires red hot, asking for you. That's how I knew you were coming. Why didn't you tell me?"

"Come with me, Aunt Margaret, while I phone. It's Olivette Hollister, my employer's sister. Stay with me," Ellen begged as she picked up the receiver.

In a few moments Olivette's clear voice lilted over the telephone.

"Ellen—Ellen dear?"

"Yes, Aunt Olivette. It's Ellen." Then, her voice thin, "Has something else happened?"

"No—Ellen, dear—no. It's just that a newspaper man got to Mary's grandfather before I could head him off and he told the reporter that you had been calling on Mary the night before her death. That got into the papers; also, that you couldn't be found, and I thought it might frighten you if you came across it unprepared."

"I did see the headlines," Ellen told her.

"I explained everything to the authorities here, and told them how you were with me the whole evening, from eight-thirty on. I said you only went to Mary's house to leave some sewing for her."

"That's true," Ellen told her.

"The medical examination showed that Mary's body had been in the water only about two hours. They found it at six, which, of course, meant she died many hours after you saw her."

Olivette stopped for breath. Oh, how matter-of-fact, even heartless, the recounting of Mary's death sounded. Yet it was all true. When Ellen didn't answer right away, Olivette called:

"Ellen, you there? You heard me?"

"Yes, oh, yes, I do hear you. And I'm so grateful to you for telling me all this."

"Everything's taken care of, Ellen. So you stay right there with your aunt and try to forget what happened. No one could have prevented any of it."

"I do thank you so much for everything," Ellen said.

"Dear Ellen, I did nothing at all except keep my head on my shoulders. Only the years can teach you that." Ellen thought she heard a soft sigh.

Then the bright voice went on, "Let me hear from you when you feel like writing. Good-bye."

When Ellen turned again to Aunt Margaret, she saw she was reading the article about the suicide. It was all over the front page—she couldn't very well miss it. But as Ellen came over to her she slapped the paper down on the couch and jumped up.

"I had time to get you a nice lunch. You sit down and eat it and then tell me what's all this." She cast a backward glance at the newspaper.

Obediently, Ellen sat down and ate a little, and began the sad story of Mary's suicide. She made reservations as to Clyde; later, perhaps, she could tell her aunt about him.

"Have you given up your job with Mr. Hollister?" Aunt Margaret wanted to know.

"Oh no. I'm still working for him. But he is not able to go on with his book right now, and I came to pay you a visit and have you back me up like you used to."

"I'll back you to the hilt, Elly, any day. If you want to work, that's all right, too. Only remember this home is always here for you; it will all be your own some day. Now tell me about your boss, Mr. Hollister."

Ellen told her about the trip to California and Paul Jean's accident; that he wasn't able to continue with his book for a while.

"He sounds like a wonderful man, Ellen. Wish I could have met him twenty years ago—sounds like a man I'd listen to."

Then Ellen got Aunt Margaret to talk about her own affairs. It wasn't difficult. As she said herself, she was simply bursting with her new project. She had always brought unbounded enthusiasm to everything she did.

"I was lonesome, Elly. This idea struck me like a shot." She got up and got a cigarette for herself and one for Ellen. Then she walked about the room, talking, delighted to have such an interested listener.

"Have a couple of dozen children from some orphan's home come out every day and play on your big, useless, beautiful lawns, I heard myself saying. So I did. Made a big thing of it, too. I've changed the ballroom that hasn't seen a ball in twenty years into a gymnasium for my precious kids. The whole second floor is now a modern nursery, where the smaller ones can have naps. Had special low tables made for the lawn where we serve all the right things for them to eat, especially milk and fruit and bread and butter. Never had so much fun before in my life."

"That's wonderful," Ellen said. She forgot her own problem in forcing herself to listen to the older woman and her plans for the children. She was glad she had come here; she would work hard, helping Aunt Margaret.

"Tell me what I can do, Aunt Margaret. I want to pitch in and help."

"You don't think you could get out of it, do you? I'm counting on you, now that you're here, for help with a special crowd that is coming out tomorrow," Aunt Margaret told her.

She was as good as her word, and kept Ellen so busy the rest of the day that the girl had no time to think of her own worries. Later Ellen remembered Mabilla, and said she wondered what her stepmother was doing.

"I'll bet she never told you I settled a small income on her," said Aunt Margaret, her eyes twinkling shrewdly.

Ellen shook her head, amazed.

"I made it a condition that she would stay away from you, never try to live with you." The older woman patted Ellen's shoulder. "There are some people who just don't belong together, and after Mabilla left here and I got to thinking how miserable she could make you if she insisted on living under the same roof with you, I decided the best thing for all concerned would be to pay Mabilla something to leave you alone! I'm fond of you, Elly."

"I love you, Aunt Margaret." Ellen kissed the older woman on her warm, soft cheek. "You're wonderful."

"I'm smart, too," retorted her aunt. "I know

enough about people to write a book. I wish I had time to write one."

There was another phone call from Aunt Olivette.

"How are you?" she caroled. And, not giving Ellen a chance to answer, "Heaven knows I don't have to ask that—all I have to do is hear the sound of your voice. You're feeling marvelous!"

"So you know," Ellen laughed.

Olivette said, with a slight catch in her voice, "I had a letter from Kurt. He said, 'Give Ellen my love.'"

Ellen thought rapidly, He wants Aunt Olivette to know about us. Scarcely able to make herself heard because of the tightening of her throat, she said, "Thank you, Aunt Olivette, for telling me."

"And there's news, in a way, Ellen, Clyde has left us. He's going to South America. Went away the day of Mary Gilly's funeral. He will be in New York, he said, a little while, and will fly from there."

A few days later she called again. "I miss you terribly, Ellen. I want someone to talk to." After a minute she said, "I was in Kurt's rooms today. I wanted everything to be in order when he gets back. I always see to it. That—that Beatrice would never take the trouble. By the way, here's something strange. I hadn't thought it was until this minute. There's a letter from Bearice on Kurt's desk: been there since last week. When Kurt phoned me from Chicago, I told him about it, and asked him if I should send it to him. He said, no—to hold it."

She hesitated again. "I mean it's strange that she should write him. They hardly ever speak to one another—why should she suddenly have to write him a letter?" After a moment she went on thoughtfully, "I haven't seen Beatrice since that night you and I met her in the gallery and I told her to stay out of Paul Jean's rooms at night and let him rest."

When the older woman paused Ellen asked, "How is Paul Jean?"

"He's screaming the house down for you, Ellen. That will tell you better than words how much improved he is. He will be able to get around in a wheel chair in about two weeks, the doctor thinks. In fact, he wants me to give you a message. He said, 'You tell Ellen I want her back here. She'll mount and ride, just you wait and see.' Doesn't that sound like him?"

"Oh, I'm so glad to hear that," Ellen said. "Of course I'll come back and finish the book, tell him. Let me know when you think he's strong enough to work on it again."

❖❖ 14 ❖❖

Ellen threw herself into every task Aunt Margaret set for her, and because there was so much to do, and such blissful fatigue at night that she could not lie awake and worry, she found the days telescoping together, and a kind of contentment settling over her troubled spirit.

The coming of the buses in the early afternoon was always exciting. Though there were always two attendants, a young man for the boys and a woman for the girls, there was enough work to keep ten pairs of hands busy, as Aunt Margaret said. She had really gone into the project thoroughly.

The American flag fluttered in the breeze over the tennis court, where big swings had been set up. The swings were always swooping up and down, full of screaming, laughing children, as soon as the wheels of the bus stopped turning. The breath-taking slide was in great demand, the children lining up automatically for the climb to the top, and taking turns slithering madly downward. It seemed incredible to Ellen that so much action could get under way in such a brief time. She ran from group to group, just as Aunt Margaret did, adjusting differences, comforting, encouraging, and picking up stray casualties.

Busy days raced by for Ellen. It was all she could do to keep up with Aunt Margaret's ideas, but Ellen reveled in it.

She and the children were playing a game one day and Ellen was standing in the middle of a circle of the children, their hands joined. They were singing, and with one line of the song they would skip in one direction around her, first to the right:

"Ring around a rosy—pocket full of posies,"

There came a sharp halt at the end of the line. The children veered left with their skipping.

"Wrote a letter to my love."

Something made Ellen glance toward the entrance to the drive; she stood transfixed. At that precise moment a shiny-nosed, low-slung roadster made a beautiful turn into the driveway, and as she stood there unable to move, it swooped up and stopped opposite her. The door burst open, and Kurt was running across the lawn. Ellen had a wild impulse to run to meet him, to sink into his embrace. But she couldn't move.

Kurt reached her, caught her fiercely to him, pressed her head down against his shoulder, and held it there with his hand. His lips against her hair, he accused, "You went away."

The circle of children had parted to let Kurt pass, but it had closed up again now and the children stood surrounding them, like so many small statues in rompers and sunsuits. Unblinking round eyes stared, in pairs.

"I had to, Kurt." Ellen had lifted her face to look up at him.

"Hush," he said, and his mouth came down on hers for a long minute. "Something has happened," he whispered as he released her. "Let's get away from this interested audience." His arm around her waist, they crossed the smooth green lawn and went into Aunt Margaret's little house.

"Oh, my darling," he began, as soon as they were inside the door, but stopped, as if he didn't know how to tell her. "Here," he said, "put your head here over my heart."

Ellen hid her face against him.

"They went away together—Beatrice and Clyde," said Kurt.

For a moment Ellen didn't feel anything at all. Then she raised her hand, put it over his where it rested on her head, and pressed her head closer to his heart. In silence he picked her up in his arms and carried her to a circular window seat at the end of the hall, overlooking Aunt Margaret's rose garden. For some moments she had neither the will nor the power to move. From the shelter of his arms she could see the rose arbor, where a few belated white roses were still blooming. While she watched, she noticed that the slight breeze was sending a shower of petals from one of the roses. They drifted downward slowly.

The pressure of Kurt's arms tightened. Suddenly, as if he had just said it, she realized what it was he had told her. It was as if she were recovering from shock. She reached up, her arms around his neck, and pressed her lips against his lean cheek.

"Kurt, I worship you. I'm not afraid to say it."

She didn't know there were tears on her cheeks until Kurt touched them with his fingers to wipe them away. "I love you truly, Ellen. I love you with all my soul, I think." He bent his head, kissed her lips, her eyes, her throat.

"It's you and I forever," he murmured. "What went before was wilful, cruel waste. My darling,

I'll live at my club until—for whatever time it takes to—to be free. Will you go home, and wait for me?"

"I'll wait, dearest. At home, with Aunt Olivette."

She smiled and held out her arms. As he came over to her, it seemed to Ellen as if he had just stepped through a dark door, that it had fallen to behind him and would never open again.